Callously offered by her Uncle Wat to Dirk Farr, the darkly mysterious gipsy laird, Kirsty Howison finds her happy girlhood abruptly halted after the death of her beloved grandfather. Her betrothed, a favourite of Mary, Queen of Scots, is rumoured to possess strange powers. Kirsty, seeking the Queen's protection, inadvertently pitches herself into still greater turmoil. Her uncanny resemblance to Mary – which deceives even the impetuous Earl of Bothwell – makes her the Queen's vital pawn in a perilous game against her powerful arch-rival, Elizabeth of England. Exactly what part Dirk Farr plays – protector or traitor – is as baffling to Kirsty as the threatening shadows that dominate the Scottish Queen's court.

The Shadow Queen

Margaret Hope

MILLS & BOON LIMITED
London · Sydney · Toronto

First published in Great Britain 1979
by Mills & Boon Limited, 17–19 Foley Street,
London W1A 1DR

© Margaret Hope 1979
Australian copyright 1979
Philippine copyright 1979

ISBN 0 263 73087 5

Filmset in 10 on 11pt Plantin

Made and printed in Great Britain by
C. Nicholls & Company Ltd
The Philips Park Press, Manchester

CHAPTER
ONE

THE tiny cavalcade toiled up the steep incline from Cramond. As they crested the hill, a fair city lay spread out before them, shrouded in early morning mist. Edinburgh, capital of a kingdom ruled over by Mary Stuart, the girl-Queen who was only a little older than Kirsty Howison, who now stood up excitedly in the leading cart.

This was the day she had long awaited. Through the cruel winter and the bitter spring of 1562, she had kept this scene firmly fixed in her mind's eye.

A dark loch, the gaunt shape of a castle huge like a crouching beast, riding swift thunderclouds with the light behind it, sharp as silver. The landscape dominated by the curve of a vast hill; Arthur's Seat, men called it, where Britain's warrior king slept through the ages, awaiting the call to deliver his land from danger and folly.

A pretty fable, thought Kirsty. And as if in answer to legend, a horseman appeared on the path below them, galloping swiftly by the waters of the Nor' Loch, to where the grey tourelles of the Palace of Holyroodhouse thrust through the drowsy morn, the palace wherein the young Queen of Scots still slept.

The sun gleamed pale upon the rider's head. Kirsty felt her heart contract. Andrew? Could it be Andrew come to meet them?

Narrowing her eyes against the light, she savoured her first disappointment of the day. The sunlight had tricked her, reflecting off the horseman's steel bonnet. His black cloak billowed in the breeze and his horse's mane too streamed silver against the light. To complete the picture of grace and speed, a huge grey wolf-hound, large as a pony, loped easil at his side. On and on towards the palace he rode; his mission, judging by his hard-ridden foam-flecked horse, was urgent.

Kirsty kept him in sight until he was engulfed by the park of Holyrood where the Queen and her royal court hunted almost daily, the leafy glades so innocent-seeming, also the haunt of fiercer animals than shy deer and hare. Many were the tales told of winter travellers attacked by wolf and bear who inhabited the darker, more secret depths.

Kirsty wondered if the hunt was the horseman's destination, for even at the distance separating them he had the look of a savage hunter, a hero from some great saga who had become lost in time and wandered by accident upon the road to Holyrood. She felt the world with its bright morning light bereft by his departure, and wished she could have seen his face, for there was about the solitary rider an illusion that he belonged to a forgotten race.

Aware that she had not heard a word of her grandfather's conversation, she shook her head. How absurd to feel deprived, to feel such a sense of loss for a stranger I will never see again, she thought, as the carts were urged, their wheels creaking, down the narrow tree-lined lanes beset by hidden springs and streams, following in the path the horseman had taken. Although the sun was not yet completely risen the larks sang for joy, and from every sweet-smelling hedgerow, Kirsty breathed in the scents of May, of the world's resurrection from the darkness and despair of winter.

A sudden tugging wind, a heavy cloud which hung above the city, had the travellers anxiously watching the sky. Was it going to rain? Kirsty groaned. Wearing her second-best gown of moss panne velvet, which well became her blonde hair under its matching caul, pearl-embroidered, she pulled the dull fustian cloak around her shoulders, deploring the necessity of hiding her finery on this triumphant entry to Edinburgh. Today she felt like a lady, like a Queen, so grand in her pretty clothes. She prayed that nothing would spoil the joy of this annual occasion, for life at Cramond, since Grandfather's illness had brought Uncle Wat and Aunt Grizel to reside at Braehead, had few causes for joy. She guessed how bitterly they resented that she was Grandfather's favourite, greatly preferred by the old man to their own vast, snivelling brood.

She darted an anxious look towards him. He seemed far from well, his colour too high, his breathing too laboured. But he was stubborn; he refused to forgo the May Day Fair which he had attended since his childhood days and which he regarded as an institution of his life and trade.

Kirsty sighed. Excited anticipation, laced with nightmares of Grandfather being unfit to travel, had deprived her of a usual healthy ability to sleep for ten hours each night. Now she too frowned at the sky, wondering as did the other travellers, if the "Queen's weather", this broken spring and the storms which rolled in eternally since Mary Stuart came to her own kingdom a year since, would continue and ruin the first May Day Fair of her reign.

As the cavalcade trotted past the palace, Kirsty glimpsed shuttered windows through the budding trees. There was no sign of activity and she felt disappointed, having hoped for some rewarding glimpse of graceful ladies-in-waiting and elegant French courtiers, perhaps even the Queen herself. Alas, common sense told her the hour was too early for folk of quality to be greeting the day. Besides, the humble citizens' May Fair meant little to a royal court whose pleasures and scandalous goings-on, hinted at by Reformation ministers, were beyond the imagination of simple country folk.

Leaving Holyrood behind, the cavalcade moved briskly towards the common pasture land, property of Edinburgh townsfolk by ancient right. This in its turn gave way to orchards bordering the residences of wealthy noblemen, since all wished to have a town house near the royal court. Grandfather deplored the expansion of Edinburgh's boundaries, murmuring that upon each visit the population increased in number, and he prophesied that no good would come of it. Soon, he grumbled, even the distant and peaceful village of Cramond would no longer be safe from "foreigners".

At last they were within the Flodden Port, waiting in line

while the contents of their carts were weighed and assessed, a small custom fee paid into the "common good" fund. For Kirsty this was a slow and wearisome business, since she feared that the rain might begin before they were properly inside the city, and she fancied that already she could hear the sounds of fiddle, fife and drum from the direction of the Lawnmarket. However, despite the threatening wind which now carried rain-banners across the horizon, the sun, entrapped by high walls, shone warmly and Kirsty produced the velvet mask like the ones worn by ladies of quality to protect their delicate complexions from the elements. She noticed that other merchants' womenfolk did likewise. Only the poorer women allowed their skins to suffer strong sun, windy weather, vulgar stares – and eventually, wrinkles.

Now the tall houses of the High Street unwound, with every other chimney belching clouds of smoke into the breeze. Even in high summer, fires were needed for cooking and as most houses had wooden fronts, sparks were a continual city hazard, unknown in quiet Cramond.

The carts were moving slowly forward and Kirsty could hardly contain her impatience, when a plaintive "miaow" from the basket at her side announced that her feelings were shared by her gift for Rose Ainslie. Lifting the lid, she took out a small blue-eyed bundle of grey fur and held him to her cheek. Rose and her parents, the tavern-keepers with whom Grandfather and she would lodge that night, would appreciate Mouser's tiny son. If he followed in his illustrious father's pawmarks, not only the mice with which they were plagued, but also rats, must beware.

"Make way – make way, there!"

The imperious command was impossible for any to obey in such congestion and confusion. Kirsty stood up in the cart and let fall her mask to stare indignantly at the troopers who, undelayed by the assessors, followed them from the direction of Holyrood, reining in with difficulty their sweating, snorting horses. Roughly clad in leather breeks and jackets, thigh-boots, coarse woollen shirts open at the neck, they were heavily armed. Eyeing the hagbut and axe that each man carried, Kirsty realised that despite the peaceful occasion, the wild fierce men of the Borders had come to town.

And their leader, whose eyes sought and found her own, was undoubtedly the same rider she had seen earlier racing solitary towards the palace. As he removed his steel bonnet and ran a hand through thick black hair, she smiled to think she could ever have imagined that he was Andrew riding forth to meet them. Even at first glance, for although the sun gleaming on steel had seemed light as Andrew's hair, the man before her was as devil-dark as Andrew was angel-fair.

He saw her smile, mistook it for boldness, and Kirsty shivered beneath his intent gaze. A sudden breeze, a darkening of the sun like an omen of disaster, blew his hair, rough but shiny as a raven's wing, across his wide brow. Heavy eyebrows met above a curved nose with dilated nostrils, broad cheekbones and, despite the hint of humour in a well-shaped sardonic mouth, the long slanting eyes turned him into a pagan warrior. Aye, she had been right about that hero-fantasy, since the man before her might have leaped straight from Grandfather's ancient tapestry of the Rape of Lucrece.

Now he leaned forward, staring boldly in her direction, and Kirsty found herself again fumbling for her discarded mask, hypnotised by the lightest eyes she had ever beheld in so dark a face. Opalescent grey or green, they shimmered like pools in a dark forest, as his steady mocking gaze, used to appraising horse-flesh – or woman-flesh – idly stripped her to the bone.

Her attention thus distracted by the troopers' leader, she was suddenly alerted to a terrified "Miaow" and a deep rumbling snarl at her side. The great grey dog which she had also seen earlier had sniffed out the basket with its dainty morsel of kitten. She turned in time to see the giant slavering jaws descend upon basket and helpless occupant as the troopers moved forward.

"Stop – stop him!"

Against the horses' hooves clattering on cobblestones and the jingle of harness, her cry for help went unheard. As did

Grandfather's warning, when she leaped from the cart and ran alongside the troopers, seizing the wolfhound by the collar as he loped along with the horses.

Gleefully he shook the basket which was being speedily demolished by such treatment and Kirsty screamed as the kitten struggled out. The dog paused an instant, growling, and Kirsty thumped him with her fists, beating at his huge head. Surprised by such an onslaught, he snarled a warning and turned savage jaws upon her, releasing the kitten, which promptly vanished under the horses' stamping feet.

With a scream, Kirsty dived after it.

"What in hell's name are you at, mistress?"

She heard the voice as she fell, the enraged dog leaping upon her, open-jawed, slavering. The next moment, with the kitten in one hand, she was lifted high into the air. In one swift movement she found herself tucked under the arm of the troopers' dark-faced leader, who was using whip and curses, both freely, upon the angry dog, which was furious at being deprived of the morsel of fur he intended for his dinner.

The troop reined in, amazed and speechless before the spectacle.

"Wha's been ridden doon?"

"Naebody we ken."

The townsfolk who had rushed to the scene, encouraged by the prospect of witnessing possible disaster and crowding the congested street, departed disappointed.

Grandfather came puffing alongside. "Put down my granddaughter. Do you hear, sir? At once!"

"Willingly, old man." And Kirsty was gently supported to her feet on the ground. "Think you I have some use for this hellcat – and her kitten?" The horseman's voice was amused. "I did but save her from my dog here. She was seeking to remove his prize, which is more than I dare risk if I am to keep all the fingers upon my hand."

"It was not your dog's prize – he stole my kitten!"

"Why do we delay now?" drawled an impudent-faced trooper. He pointed to Kirsty. "For God's love, bring her along with us. We could do with entertainment, and she is comely enough."

"How dare you?" Kirsty began furiously.

"Nay, mistress, be calm now," said her rescuer. Although his deep voice sounded stern, his eyes were laughter-brimming. " 'Tis a suggestion not ill meant." Again his eyes raked over her as if he liked what he saw.

"I – I—" spluttered Kirsty, searching for words in vain.

The horseman laughed. "I apologise for our lack of courtesy. I fear my Borderers have no fancy manners. We are used to rougher lives than gentlefolk like yourselves. We take what we want – and what pleases us." Again that appreciative glance which made her long to slap his face. "And our dogs have no better manners," he added with mock solemnity.

The rising colour in her cheeks was due no longer to outraged modesty, but to rage. How dare he address her in such a manner, how *dare* he? But even as she summoned up a biting reply, with a curt good-day and the briefest of bows he was gone, the sun gleaming on a solitary golden earring under the thick hair.

Following Grandfather back to the cart, clutching the shivering kitten and tattered basket, Kirsty realised that she was shaking with terror. Realising how narrowly she had escaped death or maiming, she hardly heard Grandfather's admonishments.

"Rescuing a kitten – all this fuss. Could have got yourself killed, lass. And all for a kitten! Mouser sires them regularly enough, a kitten is no loss." He put an arm around her shoulder. "Foolish child that you are. But you were ever thus, from babyhood – impulsive, headstrong."

Kirsty did not protest, knowing that he spoke truth. Her failing had always been never to recognise danger – until it was too late.

Now as they rejoined the line of carts moving slowly in the direction of the Lawnmarket with the kitten curled in her lap, sleeping serenely unaware of the trouble it had caused, Kirsty's escapade seemed to fill the day with omens. She had been nearly savaged by a dog, almost trampled by a horse.

And such things, she knew from the past, invariably came in threes. How could a day so begun, end in delight?

The High Street had been cleared of all refuse by special order of the magistrates, and sweetened by having its cobblestones rigorously doused by a heavy thunderstorm during the hours of the night. According to the city's well-travelled merchants, Edinburgh's "street" was already famed among those of the famous European towns. Not only paved with boulder-stones instead of being mud-packed, but wide enough to resemble a market-place, it compared favourably with other streets built with an eye to defence rather than beauty. Most were narrow, dingy evil-smelling wynds, into which the sun never had opportunity to penetrate, owing to the heights of overhanging buildings. Today from those heights banners and ribbons fluttered, adding a festive note.

To their right lay Master John Knox's fine house, gable jutting over the street, fierce and pugnacious as its owner. Today, close-shuttered, it expressed the minister of St Giles' disapproval of such frivolities as May Day Fairs, and the ungodly banqueting, wining and other deadly sins which his parishioners could be counted upon to enjoy to the full before the day expired. Repentance would come on the morrow, with accompanying punishment in the form of exceeding sore heads.

Usually they lodged overnight at Gledstane House, the home of Grandfather Howison's cousin, William Gledstane. Today the house had a closed-up, deserted air.

Master Howison sighed. " 'Twill not be the same without him."

Earlier that year, tragedy had struck when the merchant had died on board his ship en route from the Hague. Now his son Andrew was in the Low Countries settling his father's affairs. And Kirsty remembered their last meeting.

One golden day last October, Andrew Gledstane had ridden out to Cramond with his father to discuss their betrothal, and the two who had been children together, faced with the knowledge that they were full-grown, had listened, avoiding each other's eyes shyly, to this embarrassing talk of marriage.

It had restrained their easy manners and stilled their laughter. Caution crept into heedless childish pranks, putting an end to racing sticks in streams, or racing with a puppy along the banks of the tree-lined river.

Even their farewell had been tinged with awkwardness, no more teasing comments, but a stately grown-up kiss. Waiting for Andrew's father, Kirsty had whispered: "Are you happy, Andrew?"

"Aye." But his voice had been doubtful, his face unsmiling.

"Do I not please you?" she had whispered.

He had caught and squeezed her hand. "There is no other lass I would wed, none in the world I am fonder of than yourself." He had shrugged, looking towards the horizon with its line of sea, like a man who dreams of a far country. "But I would we could stay as we were."

And she was to remember the sadness in his eyes at her farewell.

"When are we to be wed?" she had asked her grandfather later.

"In a year or two. There is much to be learned in the wool trade, and Cousin William wishes Andrew to complete his apprenticeship. You too are young, lass, and I am loath to lose you."

As the days had turned into weeks and months, Kirsty forgot that Andrew's enthusiasm had been less than her own. She was to be a bride and there was much to do. She had a marriage-chest of garments to sew, bed and table linen, endless plans. Deliberately she cast from her mind Andrew's rueful leavetaking as she happily awaited his return.

Grandfather's indignant voice jolted her back to the present. He was pointing towards the windows of Gledstane House. "You see that – glass! Glass was the cause of all his ills, poor unfortunate man. He was a fit hearty soul until he gave in to this notion for glass windows. 'Twill be the death of us all."

An excess of good fortune in trading had decided Master Gledstane to follow the current fashion and replace his horn windows with new-fangled and expensive glass. He had in his turn persuaded Master Howison, against his better judgement, to do likewise.

But Grandfather could not get used to the result. "I ken not where to bide," he grumbled, "where to sit to be out of the cold or the sun. Besides, 'tis inviting trouble," he added gloomily, "leaving an empty house unprotected with only glass in its windows."

Kirsty smiled, for she thought Grandfather's fears were exaggerated, since she loved the new bright shining look of the house at Cramond. She loved the sunshine pouring through the glass, warming the cold stone walls. She looked back over her shoulder at Gledstane House, wondering when she would again set foot in its elegant rooms.

"All these other folk, sensible they are," said Grandfather, warming to his subject and nodding approvingly at the more usual Edinburgh wooden shutters with their ovals cut out through which the inquisitive householder could "keek" down at the activities in the street below. "At least this taste for glass windows is but a passing fancy, and one which, please God, will never last. Mark my word, a year or two and folk will gladly go back to sensible health-giving horn. A sore lesson for some, I fear, like my poor cousin, who will catch a fever, chilled to the very bone—"

Kirsty did not trouble to argue with him that his cousin's death at sea had nothing to do with glass windows. However, the tirade was interrupted by the "swesch" or eight o'clock drum, rat-tatting through the street, summoning the townsfolk to work. Today most of them had been about since the first streaks of dawn lightened the sky above the castle's ramparts. It reminded Kirsty that she had not only a whole empty exciting day stretching ahead like a clean slate, but also tomorrow to spend with her friend Rose, before Grandfather returned again to Cramond.

As they approached the Lawnmarket, she noticed there were many new faces in town, easily recognisable by their dark secret looks, their gaudy attire and long golden earrings. They were unmistakable in face and dress as gipsies, or

"Egyptians", who were considered a very undesirable and dangerous element by respectable law-abiding folk. Grandfather Howison squeezed Kirsty's arm warningly.

"The Farrs are come to town, in full force, I see."

Kirsty had heard of the powerful and notorious Clan Farr, gipsies whose roots lay deeper in Scottish history than the present royal House of Stuart. There had been Farrs or Faws since ever men could remember, and their story went back to the ancient Celtic folk who had inhabited this land before history was recorded. One had fought for Robert the Bruce and another had died a hero's death with William Wallace. But not only heroes were recorded; there had been black deeds in plenty. Some had left a trail of treachery, murder, arch-villainy.

"Wherever you find a King or Queen of Scots, there you'll find a Farr," went the old saying.

"Glass windows *and* Egyptians," snorted Grandfather as if one evil followed inevitably upon the other. "Why, the town is fair packed with the scum." He sighed. "What is this fine city of Edinburgh coming to, Kirsty lass, can you tell me that?"

Although Kirsty smiled sympathetically, she did not share his displeasure. The townsfolk might fear the gipsies with good reason, but she thought their presence brought life and colour to the tall grey streets. It was as if the walls were suddenly come alive, bursting with the music of fiddle, drum and fife, the laughter and excitement of the day in store, with bright trinkets glistening, gay ribbons and the striped awnings from the more sober merchants' stalls, spilling out of every dark corner.

Grandfather stepped down from the cart and relinquished it into the care of Davy, his apprentice, and Kirsty had difficulty in walking soberly at the old man's side, eyes modestly lowered, hands gently clasped, when she longed to skip and jump and run from one stall to the other. She sniffed the air; there were interesting smells too, the warm sweet smell of comfits, of heady perfumes more exotic than those emanating from horses, bruised grass and the dark earthy

smell of early vegetables. She longed to reach out and touch
the ribbons of scarlet, gold and green upon the pedlars' trays,
to taste the bright-coloured marchpane. She followed her
grandfather reluctantly to the more respectable and less colourful stalls, where merchants and guildsmen were already
displaying their wares or soberly conducting business concerning matters more weighty than trinkets and comfits.

All around them old friends were greeting each other,
merchants' wives and children, squealing with delight, or
suddenly painfully shy and hiding behind their parents.
Kirsty was told again and again how she had grown, and as if
she did not know it full well, that she was now a woman and
was time she found herself a husband.

She looked for Rose in vain, while the small children
clustered around her, each one of them begging to hold the
kitten.

At last Grandfather said: "You may go to the Ainslies and
deliver that animal while it still has fur on its back."

"Ah-h-h—" chorused the children regretfully as she hurried back towards the High Street.

"Kirsty – Kirsty!" She turned and there was Rose Ainslie
running towards her. Breathlessly they embraced. Rose was
a year younger than herself but tall for her age, and she
danced with delight as Kirsty handed the kitten to her.

"My thanks indeed, Kirsty. How could you bear to part
with him, the little beauty? I shall call him Mouser the
Second. Will you walk back to the tavern with me, for I
cannot stay long? Mam will need my help today."

Once as they struggled through a crowd of apprentices,
Rose gave a shrill cry as the kitten leaped from her arms in
alarm. Kirsty was hoping to watch the dancing bear and also
the wrestlers, which Grandfather would not have allowed,
but Rose insisted that they hurry.

"Please, Kirsty, I am afraid if Mouser escapes again I
will never recover him in this throng. Someone might steal
him."

"I almost lost him to a wolf-hound when we arrived." And
Kirsty told her of the encounter with the Borderers. "The

man with them was in uniform, very grand but strange, foreign-looking."

Rose urged her to describe it, a task Kirsty found difficult. However, she pointed excitedly to one of the banners strung across the street between the tall houses.

"The emblem he wore – a flower – like that one."

"That's the *fleur-de-lys*," said Rose knowledgeably. "Your trooper must be one of the *Garde Ecossaises*." Seeing Kirsty's frown, she explained: "The *Garde Ecossaise du Corps du Roi* or in this case *de la Reine*, since we have no king, only a queen. They are men-at-arms and archers, the Scottish bodyguard of the French kings from long since. The Queen brought them from France with her to be her special bodyguard. My Da has told me all about them," she added in tones of awe.

"This one certainly sounded Scottish."

"If he was wearing the uniform of a captain then he probably went to the French court as a boy, since many of our nobles sent younger sons to serve the French kings, especially those sons who would not expect to inherit titles or lands." Rose shivered. "Some of them are very wild indeed and they have a name for courage and fierceness – and a very bad reputation." She smiled. "The lasses, I mean, they whisper that they are very wicked lovers too. But I know naught of that, only that my Da says that if God had given him all daughters instead of sons, he would be locking them up when the Queen's guards come to the tavern."

Kirsty stifled a chuckle at her friend's doleful tone.

"And Mam too says that a lass's reputation is instantly ruined by any association with them," continued Rose. "If a respectable woman is seen in their company, then she might as well take to the taverns and earn a living on the streets afterwards, for no decent man would have her. They have their way of a lass, Mam says," she whispered, "and that is all they want. Ruthless, cruel, they are."

We take what we want. Kirsty saw again the dark mocking face of her morning encounter.

"You may be thankful that your Grandfather was with

you, otherwise he might have carried you off," said Rose in thrilled tones. "Master Knox said in his sermon last Sunday that the Queen is allowing her *Garde Ecossaise* and her courtiers to turn the palace into a royal brothel." She put a hand to her mouth, staring at Kirsty with shocked eyes. "My Da, however, says we must not believe everything Master Knox says against the Queen, for he hates her just for being a Catholic."

As they reached the tavern, Kirsty realised that she was unlikely to see the man whose strange looks had fascinated her, since his duties – and presumably his pleasures – would keep him within the palace confines. And although she would never have admitted her feelings to Rose, she felt just a twinge of regret.

CHAPTER
TWO

ALTHOUGH the tavern was not yet open, Mistress Ainslie had been busy since dawn. Kirsty found her in the kitchen with her servants, surrounded by a mountain of pies and refreshments. In the fireplace a great cauldron of soup spread its beguiling odours, reminding Kirsty that she had been too excited to break her fast before leaving Cramond.

Mistress Ainslie hugged her and remarked on how she had grown. She also sensed hunger in her daughter's friend, and thrust two bowls of soup on the table before them. When Rose protested, her mother said sharply:

"Eat! You will need all your strength this day, daughter, to help us serve out there. Appetites will be sharp and so will thirsts."

Kirsty noticed how handsomely Mistress Ainslie was dressed and as she followed Rose into the parlour, she observed new furniture, padded chairs and a tapestry; there was more silver and pewter on display than she remembered from her last visit.

Her exclamations of delight brought forth the explanation from Rose that the tavern had prospered greatly since the Queen came to Holyrood, and they had many illustrious customers from the royal court.

"Have you ever seen the Queen?" asked Kirsty innocently.

Rose laughed. "Seen the Queen? Many times – almost every day. Why, she rides up and down the street so often between Holyrood and Edinburgh Castle that folk are beginning to call this the Royal Mile. At one time I would race to the door, but now – well, it is commonplace."

"Oh, I do hope I will see her. I hear that she is beautiful as a princess from a fairy-tale."

"Aye, she is that. And the people still flock to her side, the men all in love with her, the women longing to imitate her—"

"Rose, don't stand there gossiping," Mistress Ainslie interrupted.

"I was only telling Kirsty about the Queen." Rose sounded injured.

"I dare say Kirsty will see the Queen for herself. Now, give me that kitten and I'll put him in a safe place, the wee mite will be scared to death in all the confusion. There, my precious, come to Mam. Be off with you, Rose, and escort Kirsty back to Master Howison's booth, but return directly. We shall be opening the tavern within the hour."

"Ah, Mam, let me buy some ribbons first, a comfit or two, I beg."

Mistress Ainslie smiled, for in her vast brood of sons she had but one daughter. "Very well, lass – here, for you to spend."

Rose grasped the coin she handed her with delight.

"And one for you, Kirsty." She cut short the thanks by saying: "Tell Master Howison that we have a bed prepared for him and we will expect you both to sup – earlier, if you should weary. You may share Rose's bed tonight."

In the now crowded street, the two girls met several of Rose's friends making their way to the Fair. Chattering excitedly, they wandered past the colourful exciting booths, past pedlars and fortune-tellers with dark secret faces. Some of the girls stopped to have their futures told but Kirsty, similarly invited, declined. She did not want any gipsy to spoil her own plan for the future by telling her some fanciful story, which even if she did not believe it, would worry her.

She explained this to Rose, who said: "Mam has warned me not to go near the creatures. Egyptians they are, but they do tell true." She shivered delightedly. "I have been promised a husband from over the sea, a foreigner, and six children. That should not be difficult, seeing that Edinburgh is packed with Frenchmen these days."

Kirsty was conscious of eyes upon her and, turning, found herself staring into the dark sardonic face of her rescuer of the morning. No longer accompanied by the rough Borderers, he walked with a group of young men in the same uniform as himself. The steel bonnets had been laid aside, although they wore the leather cuirass embossed with the *fleurs-de-lys*. Leather gauntlets jewelled and similarly adorned were tucked into red tartan sashes, and all wore the black velvet cloak, so handsome with its silvered facings. Under the cloak she caught a glimpse of ruff and wide sleeves, silver-slashed. The guardsmen were not alone and upon the leader's arm was a girl, young but already a tavern wench judging by the paint on her face. Her companions whispered to the other Gardes, while the girl clung voluptuously to the dark-faced leader, whispering into his face.

Seeing Kirsty he smiled, and Kirsty politely inclined her head towards him. The wench scowled, fearing competition, and tugged impatiently at his sleeve while, grimacing rudely, she stuck out her tongue at Kirsty.

As the couple turned away Rose whispered: "You did not tell me you knew Dirk Farr." Her tone was accusing and a little shocked.

"Dirk Farr? Is that his name? Then he is a gipsy?"

"Aye, and a Border laird – from Laverock, some thirty miles south."

So that accounted for the troopers who were with him earlier, thought Kirsty, the wild men of the Borders.

"His mother, who is leader of the Clan Farr, almost a queen in her own right, was second wife to Lord Laverock, a widower with one son," Rose told her. "Dirk Farr had little hopes of inheritance and his father, who had seen service with the *Garde Ecossaise* in his young days, packed him off to France. Alas, both Lord Laverock and his heir died of a putrid fever two years since. So when Dirk Farr returned from France with the Queen, it was to claim his inheritance. I dare say Mirella Farr, his mother, was not displeased by the

turn of events, for it is rumoured that she and the Clan Farr
are already firmly established in Castle Laverock. The country suits them well, for it is a wild forbidding place."

Even as the crowd swallowed the soldiers and their
wenches, Kirsty saw the dark head turn once more in her
direction, black hair gleaming and the sunlight touching the
solitary earring he wore. His glance was enigmatic – puzzled,
as if he sought to recall her face from some elusive memory.
She remembered again the strange feelings his appearance
had aroused in that first glimpse on the road to Holyroodhouse before the episode with Rose's kitten. She had longed
to meet him again – and had done so. Her wish had been
granted although under dire circumstances. Meeting him
again brought a chill of foreboding; the certainty, according
to her belief, that misfortunes come in threes, and they would
meet once again.

"They say he is a warlock," said Rose, "for his mother,
Mirella, is a known witch."

A warlock? Yes, that fitted too. Perhaps he had the ability
to conjure up her presence as he wished, Kirsty thought.
Shivering, she remembered that long glance.

"A warlock?" she repeated. "But that is a burning
offence."

"Right enough. But none can prove it, and the Queen
thinks well of him, she would never listen to slander about
her *Garde Ecossaise*. Besides, we have not had a witch-
burning in Edinburgh in my lifetime," added Rose in unmistakable tones of regret. "I fear no one worries about witches
these days, it is clear out of fashion. And our Queen tolerates
all manner of strange folks and stranger beliefs, for she has a
kind heart and a ready ear for a sad romantic tale. . . . What
news have you of Andrew?" she added. "And when does he
return from the Low Countries?"

Kirsty confessed that she had not heard from him and Rose
took her arm sympathetically. "Which probably means that
he is already on his way home. 'Twill not be long now, for
sure, especially since Gledstane House is for sale."

Kirsty stopped in her tracks, the noise of the fair vanishing under the pounding of her heart. "I did not know. When did you hear of this?"

She hardly listened to Rose's answer. Gledstane House for sale? What could that mean? Did Andrew not intend to return to Edinburgh after all? Panic surged through her. Surely he would have told her of his intention? Surely he would have written? Perhaps the letter had gone astray. A dozen reasons fluttered through her mind and were lost. Gledstane House, the home she expected to be mistress of, as Andrew's wife, to be sold!

Seeing her distress, Rose put an arm about her shoulders. "I thought you would know already – that Andrew would have written and told you."

Kirsty's eyes clouded with tears. She could think of no words to excuse Andrew's callous behaviour and thankfully said farewell to Rose, eager to sob out her news to Grandfather. But at the booth she found him heavily involved with a customer, a man of some wealth judging by his servants and elegant attire. Determined to fight off the anxiety over Andrew which threatened to ruin her day, Kirsty walked round the booths, but all that had enticed her before as gold and desirable was now tinsel and tawdry. Over and over, her mind asked the same question. Why had not Andrew written to her, telling her of his plans? And what she had dismissed as his usual indifference to putting words on paper now became ominous, sinister.

To sell the house, quit Edinburgh, with never a word to his betrothed! She could not believe he was capable of such callous deceit. Her eyes filled with tears and even the bright day darkened, for the sun had disappeared under heavy cloud, a chill wind shook the awnings and turned the town back to grey again; solidly grey, those ancient walls appearing against a greyer sky.

Returning from her aimless wandering, she found that Grandfather had vanished. In charge of the booth was Davy the apprentice.

"The master went off with milord Hamilton. I know not when he will return." Ruefully he pointed to the spots of rain descending like black coins at their feet. "I expect the rain will drive them into the Ainslie Tavern." As he spoke the spots became heavier, sending everyone flying for shelter, Kirsty among them.

At the tavern she found many others in similar plight, ruefully shaking the rain off ruined finery. She had been glad after all of the fustian cloak which she had snatched before her flight.

She searched amongst the customers hopefully for her grandfather, expecting that any moment the door would open and he would appear. At the windows others glumly considered the torrents of water racing over the cobblestones.

The May Day Fair had been ruined.

Rose abandoned the kitchen to join her friend in this vigil over the weather. Helpless they watched; there was nothing anyone could do now to save the day.

Mistress Ainslie was at her wit's end how to deal with the unexpected and sudden crowd who poured in to seek shelter and refreshment until the storm abated.

"You two lasses will need to lend Mam a hand," said Master Ainslie, passing by with a giant tray of pies.

Rose made a wry face, but Kirsty went forward willingly, delighted with the novelty of being a serving wench for an hour or two. She was also glad of an opportunity to assist the Ainslies, who always received her graciously and generously made her welcome.

Not only the humble were seeking shelter from the storm. The door now opened constantly to admit courtiers from Holyrood who had also been trapped, and Master Ainslie decided that there was nothing for it but to make available some of the private chambers to accommodate the extra customers, too fine for the tavern.

The Ainslies prided themselves upon their hospitality. While most inns were frugal affairs, offering guests the privilege of sharing a bed with several other travellers, the Ainslie Tavern offered privacy, a private bedchamber which could be hired by the night or longer and kept exclusively for the hirer's use. This caused some wry comments. Were the Ainslies getting above themselves, ye ken?

And Master John Knox, who was not unknown for his addiction to the better things in life, despite his screeching impromptu sermons upon the vileness and corruption of the royal court and its mistress, Queen Mary, decided to have a dig at his parishioners, the Ainslies, by passing mention that private beds in private chambers gave rise to a lowering of moral standards. Once the bedchamber door was locked, all manner of unseemly corruption might be calculated to take place, especially with the *Garde Ecossaise* in town, and others who followed the Catholic faith, and trailed after their Jezebel mistress from France, bringing their vileness with them.

"For a man so worthy and in league with the Almighty, I fear that Master Knox has a lewd and filthy mind," grumbled Mistress Ainslie.

Her husband agreed that the minister of St. Giles had a ready and vivid imagination upon the subject of fornication. However, as church members they discovered that Master Knox was not unwilling to share the fruits of their labours in a heavy donation to funds.

A flight of steps, the forestairs, led from the street below into the private apartments of the tavern. The noise and confusion had awakened the baby Tom, who was demanding his mother's breast at a time when she could not be spared from her labours.

Kirsty found her busily preparing sops of bread and milk which she offered to feed to the babe. The warm body held close to her heart, with tiny starfish fingers clutching at her own, made her wistful for the brothers and sisters she had never known. She was the only child of Grandfather's one beloved daughter, and her father had been a remote Howison cousin from the Highlands who had accidentally drowned several months before her birth. Her mother had succumbed to childbed fever and from that moment, Grandfather had devoted his entire life to Kirsty. A few servants too had served her with tenderness, granting her every wish; and always in the background, nodding approval, had been her gentle doting grandfather. Almost apologetically, he had tried to make up for her absence of kin, with a good measure of success.

His only son to survive infancy, her Uncle Wat, had married and stayed in Dunbar, rarely visiting Braehead, until Grandfather's serious illness that winter had brought him with his wife, Aunt Grizel, and a horde of screaming rapacious children, to take over the reins of management of the house and its policies. Grandfather had survived and grown stronger, but still they remained and in the face of these shrill ill-natured cousins, Kirsty had learned how lucky she had been through the years to live in solitary peace. Uncle Wat constantly disagreed with Grandfather, Aunt Grizel bullied the servants, many of whom left in hurt and angry protest. The odious children bickered endlessly and the once pleasant airs of Braehead, now thick with disharmony, caused Kirsty grave doubts as to whether blood *was* thicker than water after all.

She thought of those unrelated to her; Mistress Booth, Grandfather's housekeeper, who had lavished a mother's devotion upon her since her earliest days. The Ainslies, especially Rose, who was like a sister. Humble servants who were more kin to her heart than Uncle Wat, Aunt Grizel and the snivelling cousins, who were strangers in every way except for the accident of birth and marriage.

And now, gazing down at the small face of baby Tom as he cooed so contentedly in her arms, she drew him close, sighing no longer for brothers and sisters, but for a babe, a child of her own body to love and cherish. Staring into the future, she saw Andrew returning with an easy explanation for his mysterious behaviour. She saw him kissing her, laughing and with all obstacles rolled away, and they would live happily ever after. But unlike the fairy tales, her joy would not end there, for in a little while she would hold a babe to her breast, living proof of the fulfilment of their love.

Her daydream was interrupted by Master Ainslie, who ushered in two gentlemen who were foreign courtiers, judging by the amount of feathers, satin, velvets, and diamonds revealed under their elegant but rain-sodden cloaks. Both wore obvious wigs and paint on their faces.

They look like men dressed up as women, thought Kirsty, trying hard not to giggle at these apparitions from the court at Holyrood. She hoped as, hampered by baby Tom, she tried to curtsey with a solemn face, that the Queen also had good Scotsmen around her, real men of the calibre of the Borderers who had ridden into town that morning behind their laird, the gipsy Dirk Farr of Laverock. She brought his strong hard face to mind, the face of a fighter. These foolish, foppish creatures posturing before her would hardly know how to raise a sword.

With baby Tom asleep in his cradle, Kirsty at last tiptoed from the parlour to rejoin Rose and her mother in preparing vast mountains of food in the kitchen. Weariness and boredom, waiting for the rain to cease, had increased the customers' appetites and they were no longer content with ale and pies. Mistress Ainslie decided to serve an early "disjune" or luncheon; the Cock-a-leekie soup for which the tavern was famous, Friars' Chicken, made from broth of a young fowl and served with slices of the chicken, an Ashet of Pork, a Gigot of Lamb and for those who could afford it, her very special Veal Flory. All would be served with the finest manchet bread as eaten by the Queen herself in Holyroodhouse, and there were vegetable stews as side-dishes for those of coarser appetites.

"Stay you in the kitchen, Kirsty, for 'tis here you are most needed. Besides, Master Howison might not like to have his granddaughter stared at by tinkers and soldiers and the like riff-raff."

Kirsty had little time for disappointment and she even forgot that her May Day Fair had been ruined when she was swept into the good-humoured activity of Mistress Ainslie's kitchen. She could not imagine where all the hours had gone when at last the curfew drum sounded through the town warning all revellers that the hour was eight of the clock and time that all good citizens were in their beds. There was a great clamour of exodus in the tavern, since any found on the streets after sunset were liable to heavy fines, and if they were unable to pay the fine, then imprisonment in the Tolbooth.

"Off to bed, you two lasses, instead of sitting there yawning. Nay, I'll not have any excuses, daughter. I have hands enough with the servants here to make short work of getting everything spick and span before we open in the morning."

Kirsty was glad to be so dismissed, for her legs ached with weariness. "Come along, Rose," she whispered.

"Aye, daughter, vanish this instant, or your Mam will put a mop in your hand," grinned Master Ainslie.

At such a warning they left behind utter chaos, the tavern floor awash with spilt ale and worse, and in the kitchen a monument of bowls and spoons, pots and pans.

"Sleep well," said Rose's mother. "I will tell your grandfather you are abed when he arrives and you will see him on the morrow. His bed is ready and he will, no doubt, be glad to retire with a hot posset after the day's activities."

Usually the two girls talked until the early hours, but to Rose's disgust her friend fell heavily asleep in the middle of a most fascinating conversation. Fascinating that was, from Rose's point of view, seeing that it concerned a young apprentice who was paying her particular attention.

As for Kirsty, she was too tired even to dream. However, she awoke some time during the night to hear a door close, footsteps, and thought with relief that Grandfather must have arrived. The rain still lashed the windows, and with a twinge of anxiety, she hoped that he would not be too tired to send his clothes down to the warm kitchen to dry overnight. After his recent illness, the exhaustion of a long day completed by a thorough drenching could be serious indeed.

I should go and make certain that he is warm and comfortable, she thought. I should go— But her limbs refused to obey the command and she knew no more until Mistress Ainslie was throwing back the shutters and Kirsty thankfully awoke from a disquieting dream wherein Andrew's fair face persisted in changing into the devil-darkness of the light-eyed *Garde Ecossaise*, Dirk Farr.

"Wake up, my lassies," said Mistress Ainslie. "You have slept overlong and even the Queen is up and abroad before you. Think shame to lie in your bed while Her Majesty rides so urgently down the street. Quick, she is within sight now."

At the news of her monarch's approach, Rose groaned and turned on her side, but the excited shouts and footsteps running past the tavern had the effect Mistress Ainslie desired, since Kirsty leaped from bed to stand on tiptoe on the tiny balcony overlooking the street.

"It's the Queen, Rose – do come and see her."

From the bed Rose groaned again. "Not I. Tell her, Mam, I see the Queen practically every day. Oh let me be, for I am weary."

Kirsty was long to remember her first sight of Mary Stuart, Queen of Scotland and the Isles. In black velvet gown with fur-trimmed riding cloak, upon her head a small hood of lawn wired to form a wide curve with a dip above the centre of her forehead, and over that a "bongrace" of stiffened velvet falling from the hood to her shoulders and thus protecting face and neck from sun and wind. She clasped the white horse's reins in gauntlet gloves, richly jewelled, the green of emerald and red of ruby gleaming in the morning sunlight. As the sudden breeze caught her bongrace, Kirsty had a glimpse of tight-curled bright auburn hair.

" 'Tis a peruke," Rose said knowledgeably. She had appeared by her side on the balcony. " 'Tis the fashion from France that ladies and court gentlemen too wear perukes during the day, or to go out of doors when their own hair is unadorned. I am told that her hair is red-gold, fine as silk and very beautiful."

Kirsty was enchanted by the sight of a mere girl, beautiful and yet so regal. A girl who still looked like a Queen or a princess from a fairy-tale moving flower-like among the pale petals who were her four Maries, riding about her. In green velvet riding-costumes, they too presented a delightful portrait, their pretty faces, all so different, a perfect frame and adornment for their lovely Queen. Mary Seton, Mary

Beaton, Mary Livingstone and Mary Fleming had become almost as famous as the sovereign they served so loyally.

The cavalcade trotted briskly past, since this was not a state occasion, and Kirsty had little more than a quick look at the Queen's face. Why did the sight send such a sudden chill through her, she wondered, as if this moment had happened before? Why should the Queen's face bring such a sense of familiarity?

"And what think you of our Queen?" asked Mistress Ainslie. "Is she not—" Suddenly her voice faltered, she seized Rose's arm, and Kirsty, startled but smiling, saw the two pairs of eyes widen in amazement before her.

"In God's holy name," whispered Mistress Ainslie, "I have never realised—" Rushing forward she took hold of Kirsty's face in one hand and with the other swept back the hair from her forehead in a tight knot. "Do you see it now, Rose?"

Rose nodded, for once bereft of speech. It was Kirsty's turn to be frightened. What did they see on her face? Were there blotches, was she showing the first terrible signs of the pestilence?

"What is amiss?" she wailed. "What has happened to me?"

"There now, naught is wrong," said Mistress Ainslie, putting an arm about her. " 'Tis just that with your hair pulled back – so – you look like the Queen. Except that you are blonde and small and she is red-headed and tall."

"Oh, is that all?" Kirsty laughed. "I thought it to be some more serious matter."

"You are her image," said Rose, still taken aback.

"I told you so before, daughter, and your father too. I said when I first saw Her Majesty, why she is just like Kirsty Howison. But I suppose you weren't paying attention as usual," she added severely.

Rose ignored the reproof. "I never noticed it, truly, until now. And to think I have known you all these years!"

"I wonder if the Queen noticed it too?"

But speculation was cut short by baby Tom's screams as he

demanding his breakfast. Unfastening her bodice, Mistress Ainslie left them, and Kirsty, throwing a robe about her shoulders, said:

"I must awaken Grandfather."

The bedchamber was empty, the bed undisturbed. Kirsty felt sudden panic. Where had the old man been all night, in that terrible storm? She found Rose brushing her hair before a steel mirror and cried out that Grandfather was missing.

"Nay, Kirsty, your fears are groundless. 'Twas a coarse night, Master Howison was with milord Hamilton. Doubtless they gave him shelter and a bed. He will be here directly, you wait and see." Rose put down her hairbrush. "Perhaps Da will know—"

Kirsty rushed downstairs and with her hand raised to tap on the parlour door, she heard Mistress Ainslie's voice.

"Kirsty and the Queen could pass for sisters, husband."

"Perhaps there is some truth in the rumour," came Master Ainslie's voice.

"Aye, King Jamie, the Queen's father, always had an eye for a bonny lass, and after Jock Howison rescued him from the brigands and was given Braehead as a reward, ye'll mind, His Majesty oft returned to Cramond. He called it the sweetest spot in his kingdom," she added proudly.

There was a pause before Rose's father asked: "Was there not some mystery about Kirsty's father? Distant kin, was he no'?"

"So they said." And Mistress Ainslie's voice warmed to a nice piece of gossip. "Drowned too, afore Kirsty's birth, so none at Cramond ever set eyes upon him, and Jock Howison's daughter, who allegedly eloped, returned to Cramond a widow." She sighed. "She didna survive along either, poor creature." In the small silence that followed, Kirsty imagined a knowing look exchanged within the room.

"Just fancy, husband, our little Kirsty, whom we have kenned all her life, might be the late King of Scotland's daughter, half-sister to our Queen."

The idea was so outrageous that Kirsty wanted to laugh out loud. Had all this rumour arisen because she had been orphaned at birth, her father a stranger, while the King had been a constant visitor to Braehead out of liking and gratitude to her grandfather, for once saving his life? She frowned. Did others than the Ainslies give credence to such a rumour? Was that why everyone at Braehead, all the servants and her tutors, even occasional visitors, treated her to such respect, why their eyes considered her so sharply? Did that account for the strange tight-lipped silences of Mistress Booth when Kirsty enquired further about her parents?

She felt laughter bubbling inside. It was ridiculous and she longed to rush in to the Ainslies and assure them that it *was* nonsense. Alas, this was to be her last desire for mirth for some time to come.

Even as she paused with her hand raised to the door, she heard the outside door behind her burst open.

Davy the apprentice rushed in. His face was white, his manner urgent. "Oh, Mistress Kirsty, Mistress Kirsty—"

The Ainslies appeared from the parlour and Kirsty no longer cared that they must know she had overheard their conversation.

Davy fought to get his breath back, gasping: "Mistress Kirsty, you are to come – at once. The Master – has been taken ill—"

"Take me to him, quickly!"

As she raced after the apprentice, stricken that her fears for her grandfather had come true, the lad gasped out the remainder of his story. Master Howison had left Lord Hamilton at his house and was hurrying uphill here to the tavern when he gave a great cry and fell senseless to the ground. A gentleman who was entering Gledstane House, took him in—

And as she ran up the forestairs Kirsty remembered that but a short while ago she had been distressed to hear that the house was for sale. What did it matter now, with Grandfather ill, perhaps dying? Such agony over Andrew's mysterious behaviour seemed foolish and unnecessary.

An old woman, a gipsy by her dark face and dishevelled appearance, barred their way, chattering at them in some foreign tongue. But Davy pushed her aside and led the way upstairs to the guest bedchamber, which had housed her grandfather on happier visits.

"Grandfather!" she cried, for he lay on the pillows, his face purpled and the veins distended, blotched. As she knelt beside him, she heard a man's footsteps on the stairs. For a moment she wondered giddily if Andrew had indeed returned from the Low Countries, his presence most opportune now that Grandfather had been struck down.

She blinked against the light streaming through the open door and the tall figure silhouetted there. But the man who entered was not fair of face like Andrew. He was devil-dark for all his pale opalescent eyes. And they had met before.

"So the lad found you in time – I fear you are almost too late." Bowing over her hand, he said: "I am Dirk Farr, Lord Laverock – and the new owner of this house."

CHAPTER
THREE

"HAS Master Howison other kin who should be sent for?" Dirk Farr asked her gently.

"A son, Walter, presently at Braehead." Seeing his questioning look, Kirsty added, "In Cramond Village."

Dirk Farr turned to the apprentice Davy, who was hovering by the door. "Go, lad, at once, and bring Master Walter here. And call upon the physician three doors down in Mariners' Wynd. Request him to return to us at once. . . . Would your grandfather wish to have a priest?"

"A priest?" Kirsty, dazed with grief, realised that the new owner of Gledstane House was briskly taking over. She was not ungrateful, for her mind refused to accept that in the bed before her, Grandfather, beloved Grandfather who had cherished her every day of her life, who loved her as no other could or would, she thought, was already slipping from the shackles of his long life.

"Was your grandfather of the Old Faith?" When Kirsty stared at him, he added: "Was he Catholic, mistress? If so," and here he lowered his voice although there were no others present, "if so, I can get a priest from Holyrood, to give him the last rites. But this must be done secretly."

"Nay, sir – but thank you. He was of the Reformed Church. A good man, he needs no helping hand to guide him to his Maker."

Dirk Farr nodded and swung the velvet cloak across his shoulders. Taking up the steel bonnet from a chair, he said: "I fear I must leave you to your vigil, for I am on personal guard to Her Majesty and should have presented myself at her apartments an hour since. I was leaving the house when I encountered your grandfather."

"I am grateful to you—"

He cut short her thanks. "If you need assistance, Eunice there," he pointed to the old servant who now occupied the doorway, "Eunice knows only Romany and is somewhat deaf, but she has remarkable powers of understanding most folk, if they speak slowly and supplement their requests with signs. That is, if she has a will to do so."

Fearfully Kirsty considered the old woman with her baleful face.

"I have asked her to remain here with you, for she is used to nursing sick folk – and attending to other doleful matters." Seeing Kirsty's stricken expression, he continued, "She will do as you tell her, although she has no liking for Gorgios."

"Gorgios?"

"Aye." He laughed, throwing back his head, and she saw for the first time that his teeth were beautiful, strong and white against the dark face, the well-shaped lips. She looked away hastily, as he added: "Gorgios are people like yourselves, who are not Romanies but are our sworn enemies."

"I am no man's enemy," she said indignantly, fighting back tears, "and I am indebted to you for not leaving my grandfather in the street to die."

"As men like him would have left a Romany." Dirk Farr's voice was bitter.

"No God-fearing man would behave thus, sir."

"Would he not? Let me tell you I have seen this happen many times. Women too, left to die with babes in their arms, in hedgerows like starving vermin." He pointed to the old woman who watched them motionless. "Such was the case with her daughter, who was used by a Gorgio and when he had done with her kicked out like a cur dog. And there were others who could curdle your blood, mistress, with worse stories." He laughed harshly. "Be not surprised if Eunice has little love for Gorgios."

"We are not all alike. There are good Christian folk who would not pass by, there are good Romanies too, like yourself, who have compassion."

He held up his hand. "Spare me the story of the Good

Samaritan, for I know it already. Tell it to those who persecute us, who drive the Romanies from towns because our complexions are darker and our ancient ways are different." With a shrug, he picked up his gloves. "But I weary you. I shall take my leave now. Please consider the house your own until I return. There is food in the kitchen. And wine in plenty – if Eunice has not drained the barrel. She drinks overmuch sometimes."

"Sir, one more favour, if you please. Our friends at the Ainslie Tavern will be anxious. Would you be kind enough to have a message sent and beseech my friend Rose to come to me?"

"I will do so." Dirk Farr bowed, the door closed and he was gone. He moved, she thought, with a supple cat-like grace, like a man who is used to stalking prey, the stealth of the hunter, this *Garde Ecossaise*, who was also the Romany Lord of Laverock. His presence frightened her, his talk about Romanies and the injustices served upon them by good Christian folk, upset her. She was glad to be alone.

But not for long. The door opened again to admit the old woman who moved soundlessly on bare feet across the room and took a seat by the bed, staring down into Grandfather's face. Apprehensively Kirsty watched her. She seemed incredibly old, toothless, wizened, ancient beyond the mortal count of years. Her arms and hands were like gnarled twisted branches, tough as heather roots and unrecognisable as the once soft flesh of woman. Kirsty instinctively touched her own arms and wrists with their delicate bloom, their warmth. Surely they could never wither with age like the crone's before her?

As though realising Kirsty's thoughts, Eunice turned to stare at her contemptuously, muttering under her breath. Hastily, Kirsty looked away out of the window, her scalp crawling with fear. Was she being cursed?

Now the old woman rose to her feet, and bustled back and forth by the bedside, tearing back the covers and moving Grandfather's arms and legs, touching his still face with her grimy hands. Such behaviour was too much for Kirsty's sensitivity. The idea of that filthy old crone resting her hands upon her grandfather, defiling him with her odious presence, disgusted Kirsty. She said loudly:

"I will stay and do what has to be done. You may – go—" she added, accompanying the words by stabbing a finger in the direction of the door.

The woman listened carefully and nodded vigorously as if she understood every word. Soundlessly she scurried out of the bedchamber, leaving Kirsty to her lonely vigil, interrupted only by the arrival of the physician who, after examining Grandfather briefly, shook his head.

"Is he – will he recover? Is he better than when you last saw him?"

There was no reassurance, no indication of the miracle she craved in the physician's solemn face. He shook his head. "There is naught I can do, mistress. His condition has worsened. He will not come back to his senses now."

"Can you do nothing for him – nothing?" Kirsty cried out.

"Nay, but fear not, he is in no pain, he will merely sleep himself into eternity."

As he turned towards the door, Kirsty held out her hands beseechingly.

"Please – please, sir, do not leave me – so helpless. Stay—"

"I cannot stay. The living need my services," he reminded her sternly. "You would do better to pray than to weep, for that is all any can do for him now."

After he left Kirsty went to the bed and crying, covered her grandfather's face with her tears, but still he did not move. Time passed almost without her knowledge, until suddenly she wondered why Rose had not arrived.

Occasionally she heard voices from the kitchen below. Once a door closed loudly, but although she hoped it was Rose, her friend did not appear, Rose, it seemed, had deserted her, and she was left with only the storm, whose intensity had revived. Battering the windows, it turned what little light remained into gloomy dusk. Soon only the white pillow gleamed beneath the bed-curtains, framing the almost skeletal outline of Grandfather's head with its crest of white hair.

Once his lips moved and she bent closer. "I am here – I am here."

His eyes rolled away from her.

"Can I get you aught, dearest?" She thought his cracked lips moved and he murmured:

"Water – water?"

Rushing to the door, she shouted for Eunice, but none came to answer her call. Returning to the bedside, she reassured him that she would shortly return, but in the kitchen she found the gipsy woman snoring over a fire, an empty cup beside her. The air was heavy with stale wine fumes and, disgusted at the sight, she took fresh water from the barrel.

On her way back she shook the old woman, who opened her eyes, cursing and muttering in Romany.

"Fetch the Ainslies – from the tavern," Kirsty fitted the action of drinking to the words. "Please – my grandfather – I must go to him."

Again the old woman nodded vigorously as though in complete understanding, but even as Kirsty hurried upstairs, she saw her sinking back into her chair, eyes closed, mouth open.

Returning to the bedchamber, Kirsty noticed that she no longer had the house to herself, and realised that many of the noises she had heard must have been made by the cats who now followed her curiously, mewing at her heels. She lost count of how many cats slithered across floors, lurked on top of presses or under tables, climbed the stairs before her and yowled from dark corners.

Where had they come from? Did they belong to Eunice or to Dirk Farr? The Gledstanes had owned only one comfortable fat tabby cat, old beyond mousing. But these cats might have been of a different breed. All were uniformly black with pale green glittering eyes which she felt bore a remarkable and somewhat uncomfortable resemblance to the new master of Gledstane House.

She shivered, for like most folk, she had been weaned on stories of witches and warlocks who had black cats as their familiars and she had wisely lived in terror of ever meeting such a creature. Handsome Mouser, grey and soft, was a far cry from these thin cats with the eager faces of starved hunters.

Outraged, she shooed them out of her grandfather's bed-chamber as they tried to sidle in after her. Closing the door, she discovered that her heart was beating uncomfortably loudly. But not loudly enough to hide the deep sigh from the bed.

With a cry she ran forward, touching the sunken face before her, pale as the pillows on which it rested.

"Oh Grandfather – dearest," she wept, her hand enveloping fingers like old ivory upon the counterpane.

His eyes jerked open. "Is that my little princess?"

"It's Kirsty, Grandfather – your Kirsty."

He sighed. "It grows dark, lass, will no one light the candles?"

Kirsty looked at him in anguish, for the storm had passed over and now bright sunlight streamed like a cheerful blessing through the windows. She nodded and whispered: "Aye, dearest. As you wish."

But as she made to move, he gripped her hand. "Nay, lass, do not leave me." And smiling unseeing in her direction, he whispered: " 'Tis good to have you here by my side, for I love thee as no other in my life. You are truly a king's daughter, my little princess."

And with a fluttering sigh, his eyes closed upon her for ever.

At that moment, as if conjured up by magic, Dirk Farr appeared at her side. She gave a great cry and would have fallen had he not taken her into his arms and held her fast. For a while it seemed that her senses, unable to accept this grievous loss, had vanished. Then suddenly she stretched out her arms and encircled his neck, burying her face against his throat, clinging, sobbing like the helpless child he suspected she was.

It was this gesture of trust and longing more than any other which reached out and touched him deeply, this gipsy laird whom so many women desired in vain. Trust and tears. He was unused to tears. His mother never cried, nor did the gipsy women who had been his early contacts with the act of love. They never wept, all were made of the same tough steel as the Border men who had sired them.

He held her against his heart like a captive bird, whispering words in his Romany tongue that she could not understand, but although she knew not their meaning they reached her desolation, and through the mortal storm of sorrow, she knew the words were gentle, comforting and wise. Aware that her sobbing had ceased and that her great eyes implored him like a creature of the forest glade he knew so well, a great yearning for her filled Dirk's wild heart. Terrible, he thought, that her heartbreak should be his awakening to joy.

As for Kirsty, she knew only that she wanted to stay there for ever, safe and warm in those strong arms, like a barrier between herself and the sad world outside them.

Aware of another voice, that of the old servant chattering shrilly in Romany, she sat up and attempted to dry her eyes and blow her nose. Composure partly regained, she found Dirk Farr upon his knees beside her. Smoothing back her hair, he held her face between his hands and smiling, kissed her brow as if she was naught but a stricken child. Then he stiffened.

"You are kind, sir," she began, suddenly embarrassed by the intensity of his gaze.

Dirk Farr was not listening. "You are her image," he whispered.

"Whose image?"

"Why, the Queen's, of course."

Kirsty shrugged. She had forgotten the amazement expressed by Mistress Ainslie and Rose that morning when the Queen passed by Gledstane House, the morning which now belonged to a lost, happy world. She could hardly bear to glance towards the bed where her Grandfather lay, and she wished with all her heart that she could be with him on that mysterious journey into the unknown, for now she was alone. Alone.

She was too upset to appreciate the obvious admiration in Dirk Farr's eyes. Admiration, and an odd expression which she could not identify.

"It is a very singular thing to so resemble the Queen," he added, conscious of her questioning look.

The old woman thrust a goblet of liquid towards Kirsty and she pushed it away.

"Drink!" commanded Dirk Farr.

She did as she was told, choking over the fiery liquid which burned her throat.

"I have requested Eunice to bring a bowl of soup, for she tells me you have not eaten this day. Small wonder that you should take so ill," he added reproachfully.

Kirsty did not inform him that she had not been offered food, and even had she been hungry enough to require nourishment, the old woman had spent the hours of his absence in drinking herself into oblivion. And now she winced away from the few spoonsful of skink soup, coarse and inedible after Mistress Ainslie's offerings at the tavern. Revolted by its greasiness, she thrust away the spoon.

"If you will not eat, then you must rest," said Dirk Farr. "I have instructed Eunice to make up a bed for you."

"I will not stay here, sir, I will return to the Ainslies," she looked towards the bed, "in due course, when my uncle arrives from Braehead. Until then, I shall remain with Grandfather."

"And I must return to the palace within the hour. I came but to see how you fared. Do you wish someone to stay with you, a friend perhaps?"

"Rose Ainslie—"

"Has she not come? I had the message sent before I left. A lad who was passing by—"

Kirsty shook her head. Either the lad had failed in his mission or Rose had deserted her, had not wished to come. She would remain alone then, although she felt bitterly hurt by such neglect, which was far from being in keeping with

Rose's compassionate nature. Nor was it like Mistress Ainslie to abandon her in this manner, when she most needed comfort.

A short while later she had the explanation. Master Ainslie arrived at the kitchen door and without awaiting answer to his summons stormed through the house until he found her.

"Kirsty, my dear child!" He took her sobbing into his arms and said: "I am indeed sorry. And to think that you should have had to endure such a sorry business alone. 'Twas not of our knowing, for Mistress Ainslie and Rose have in their turn been refused, sent packing by this old crone," he added angrily, nodding towards Eunice who somewhat breathlessly trailed behind him upstairs, plucking at his sleeve, making it plain that she would not have admitted him, that he had no business here.

"Get you gone," he said, raising his fist. And when she meekly departed, he continued, "Rose was most upset and my good wife is fearful for your safety, so I have been sent to take you back with me."

"I cannot – I cannot leave Grandfather until my uncle arrives."

Master Ainslie nodded. "If you are afraid, I will send one of the servants."

"Nay, sir. I am not afraid of my dearest grandfather. He never harmed me in his life for he truly loved me. Why should he then wish to harm me now?" Kirsty smiled sadly. "Alive or dead, I am certain his love endures and that at this moment he still watches over me."

Master Ainslie's eyes flickered uncertainly towards the still figure. He admired Kirsty's courage, for few girls of her age would have stayed in solemn wake alone with the dead, however beloved.

After he left, Kirsty made herself as comfortable as possible in the one padded chair that the bedchamber contained. She closed her eyes wearily, and as if her grandfather truly did watch over her, she slept peacefully and without dreams until daylight filtered through the shutters, and the sound of horses, the rumble of wheels on the cobblestones outside, had her instantly alert.

Uncle Walter had arrived. She heard footsteps on the stair. The door opened to admit him, closely followed by Dirk Farr.

Her uncle greeted her formally as always, and within minutes he had, with but one cursory glance at his father's deathbed, taken complete charge of the arrangements. His manner, untroubled by natural grief over a beloved father, untouched by the wiping away of one sentimental tear, suggested to Kirsty that he might well have been awaiting this moment – nay, even planning for this woeful occasion, for some while.

"Your Aunt Grizel has most generously sent you a mourning gown. It is valuable and belonged to her younger days, when she was less stout. Put it on at once," he frowned, "for that green gown is disrespectful to the dead."

Of black velvet, old-fashioned and threadbare in places, the gown fitted Kirsty ill and she shuddered from its musty smell. However, she had neither heart nor opportunity to set to work upon the alterations which were necessary. She decided that they had thought of everything as she observed a handsome coffin being carried upstairs, from the cart, to take Grandfather on his last journey home.

Her uncle had invited her to accompany him into the adjoining chamber while the Braehead servants prepared her Grandfather's body. Dirk Farr stood silently by the door and her uncle said cheerfully:

"I would have a word with you in private, my lord Laverlock. Leave us, niece, we will call you when our business is at an end."

Kirsty wandered into the hall and stared out of the windows on to the High Street. In all probability after this day, she would never again enter this house which held such hitherto happy memories of Andrew and his father. Once she had dreamed of being mistress of Gledstane House, such a little while ago for a dream to die so sharply. She recalled other days of sitting in the window embrasure of this spacious

chamber with Andrew, while their elders talked solemnly by
the fire. And if ever she had grown tired of watching
Andrew's dear face, or their eyes strayed from the excitement
of childlike wonder at the many and varied passers-by in the
street, she had marvelled at the panels of tapestries, deco-
rated with foliage and flowers, of small animals with lifelike
expressions, peering out at them. Squirrels and monkeys
clambered along branches, while the white tails of conies
disappeared into the safety of burrows. A wind from the
chimney could then – as now – send the whole scene shaking
into a wonderful semblance of life.

She could not bear this chamber of memories and wandered into the corridor which overlooked the hall below, a
handsome stone fireplace supporting the Gledstane family
arms, the walls furnished with tapestries depicting stern
Biblical themes. Against this background of harmonious
colour, a large chandelier hung from the ceiling. Another
memento of Master Gledstane's bizarre taste and new
extravagance, Grandfather had grumbled. It was of brass
with tall white candles, and he had estimated that the
upkeep and constant replenishment of such illumination
would drive his friend into the poorhouse, for even sheep-
tallow candles at Braehead were kept under close scrutiny
and in short supply.

Numerous chests, richly carved, lined the walls and
among them stood a compt-burd or counter, upon whose
numbered squares the merchant made his calculations and
daily counted up the income from his trade. When it was not
in use, as now, it served to display his silver and large
serving-dishes. At the doorway was a "stand of harness",
armour with steel bonnet and two-handed sword, since
membership of the merchants' guilds required that all be
good men-at-arms, ready to ride out and serve Her Majesty
the Queen or take instant arms in defending the city of
Edinburgh from violence.

"Mistress Howison."

She gave a little cry as Dirk Farr stared into her face, for
she had not heard him approach. "Your uncle will receive

you now," he said and hurried downstairs without a further glance in her direction.

Wearily she returned to the chamber, shuddering to think, as she curtseyed, what the future held in store at Braehead, under the jurisdiction of such a cold austere man as Uncle Wat.

"I am ready to leave now," she said. "My cloak is upstairs."

"Leave it then, for it will not be required."

"But the weather, Uncle – 'tis a long journey—"

He shook his head. "You will not be requiring your cloak, niece, since you are to remain here at Gledstane House."

"Remain here?" And for a single instant, her heart thudded with joy. Andrew had returned to reclaim ownership of the house, that must be it. A second later realisation dawned that imagination had played her false and that no convention would allow her to remain here with Andrew until, at least, the formal handfasting approved by both sets of relatives.

"Am I to be handfasted then?"

Could that be the reason? She guessed that Aunt Grizel had never wanted her presence at Braehead even when her grandfather was alive. The custom of handfasting would suit the rapacious couple well, since the betrothed pair would by common consent, and usually most eagerly, live together for a year and a day. If at the end of that period, they were both still of the same mind, or if she were with child, then marriage would follow.

Uncle Wat regarded her with amazement. "Aye, you are, niece."

She clasped her hands with delight. "Then Andrew *has* returned. When did he come? When shall I see him?"

"Andrew?" Her uncle's face was a study in bewilderment. "Ah, niece, I see who you mean, young Gledstane, is that it?"

"Aye, Uncle."

He shook his head. "I know naught of the lad."

"But you say I am to be handfasted." Kirsty's hand flew to her mouth, at a suspicion so terrible, so vile, that she dared not give it a name. In that instant she remembered that Uncle

Wat was her guardian, her disposal was within his hands.
Her disposal wherever and to whomever he cared.

"Aye, niece, you are to be handfasted. That is my wish."

Suddenly his loathsome countenance was split by a grin as
he saw the question hovering in her terrified eyes. He chuckled.

"To my lord Laverock."

CHAPTER
FOUR

KIRSTY heard her own voice screaming: "Never – nay, Uncle – never." Then she was down on her knees, clutching the hem of his cloak. "Please, Uncle Wat, please, for dear Grandfather's sake, do not treat me thus."

He pulled his cloak away from her as though her touch defiled him. "Rise, niece. Cease this absurd behaviour."

She did as she was told and looking into his hard mask of a face she said: "What have I ever done to you or to yours, that you should treat me thus?"

"You are being foolish, niece. I have done you a favour and you should be grateful instead of weeping."

"A favour, Uncle? I do not know Lord Laverock, this man you would have as my husband."

"Then you are no worse off than a thousand other lasses. Aye, better than most, for he is a man of high social position, well regarded by Her Majesty the Queen."

Kirsty shook her head. "He frightens me," she whispered. "Besides, 'tis Andrew I love."

Ignoring her distress, her uncle walked to the window and stood staring down into the street. She thought of the cheerful voices below, the sounds of everyday life. Would she never again be free?

"I am your guardian," Uncle Wat reminded her sternly. "I can dispose of you as I wish and to whom I wish. It is most fortunate that my Lord Laverock has looked kindly upon you and is satisfied with the small 'tocher' I am prepared to give."

She knew that her grandfather had meant her to have a large dowry, and suspected that his will had been altered by them. That could be the only reason. She wondered what other iniquities they were perpetrating in her grandfather's name.

"Think of the advantages. You will have a title and this fine house. And Castle Laverock besides, if you please my lord."

"You talked of handfasting, not of marriage."

"Marriage will follow," he said smoothly. "Handfasting is my lord's wish, since it will not legally bind you, should either of you wish to change your minds."

A trial marriage of one year to a man she did not love. Who would want her then?

"Besides," her uncle continued. "My lord is a member of the *Garde Ecossaise*, personal bodyguard to Her Majesty. Where could one like yourself – an orphan – hope to find such a match? You should be crying tears of gratitude, niece, rather than behaving in this outrageous, vixenish manner."

"I know him not. We have scarcely spoken to one another. I am – afraid."

"Afraid? Why, niece? He is a gentleman, and comely too."

"He is – a Romany – an Egyptian," she whispered.

"Is that why you are fearful?" His laugher was coarse. "I dare say my lord is none the less a man for all that." And he rubbed his hands delightedly. "I think we have done well in this day's work for your future, niece. Some day you will thank me for it. Had my lord not questioned me before I left, I might have found it difficult in Cramond to arrange a match for you. A yeoman farmer would have been the greatest of our hopes."

"Then let me return with you now. I will come to Braehead as a servant. I do not care if you do not find me a husband—"

"There is no place for you at Braehead," he interrupted briskly. "Aunt Grizel and I have decided to sell the Dunbar house and take over my rightful inheritance. We have children enough of our own, daughters in plenty, I need not remind you, to find husbands for, to provide for."

"Will my lord Laverock not take one of them?"

" 'Tis true, I offered him Bess, who is your own age,

prettier and more docile too," he scowled. "But my lord would have none of her. It seems that he has taken a particular liking to you."

"He does not know me," she began.

"And I hope he will never find out what an ill-natured ungrateful wretch you are, niece. Again I remind you that you are no worse off than brides who meet their husbands for the first time at the altar. And you are not even there yet. You are not committed utterly. If in a year there is no – er, issue – and he does not want you, you will be free to seek another husband and he another wife."

"And who would want me then, Uncle? No respectable man—"

He avoided her eyes. "Come, niece, you exaggerate. There are men who would not quibble that you had been hand-fasted. For I dare say if my lord does not want you, then he will settle money on your future. Money can influence men in such matters. Some will not worry greatly if there is money at stake."

"And a tarnished bride?"

"You will be no worse off than a widow in men's eyes. But I will hear no more of this. The bargain is settled. My lord has signified his willingness to wed you, should you both be of the same mind at the end of a year."

"I am not of the same mind even before we begin," retorted Kirsty. "So how fares your handfasting, when one of the pair is unwilling?"

He stood over her in a threatening manner. "I warn you, niece, tax not my good nature, nor my lord's generosity. He regards you already with affection, and should you behave in docile manner, he will make you his wife."

"Never, Uncle, I will leave him at the earliest opportunity."

He seized her arm and shook her, so that she cried out. "Heed my warning. Should you try to run away and so belittle me in my lord's eyes, then I will proclaim your disobedience publicly and sell you as bond-woman. And if none will take you, then you shall go to the orphan asylum."

"There is one matter you have overlooked, Uncle, in your eagerness to dispose of me," she said desperately.

"Oh, what is that?" His tone was nervous.

"I am already betrothed. To Andrew Gledstane. It was arranged by Master Gledstane and my grandfather in October. There was a bond—"

"There was not. No document of such a nature exists at Braehead."

"Then you have destroyed it!"

"Watch your vile tongue, niece. No betrothal document ever existed. As you will recall, two days after the Gledstanes' visit, my father took a seizure of some sort and the bond was never drawn up, never signed. It would have been had Master Gledstane not died, I dare say. But now both the guardians are dead and Andrew Gledstane is abroad. Who knows when, or if, he will ever return to Edinburgh? And should he do so, whether, in the light of these new events, he will still wish to marry you."

They were interrupted by a servant who announced that all was in readiness for Master Howison's departure. Kirsty ran forward and clung to her grandfather's coffin as it was carried downstairs by the servants. Brutally, her hands were torn away by her uncle. She was thrust back into the parlour and she heard his voice shouting:

"Lock her in. Turn the key there."

Sobbing, she ran to the window and as she stood on the tiny balcony staring down at them, she thought for a moment of leaping down to end the sorry life which had collapsed in ruins about her.

She felt helpless, desolate, afraid and heartbroken. There was no longer one beloved old man to whom she could run and there were no words in the world to change her uncle's inflexible decision, which she now guessed had been made, with her aunt's connivance, long before he departed from Braehead. As soon as the summons came that Grandfather lay ill in Edinburgh, they must have decided that in the event of his death, Kirsty should never return to Braehead. If the betrothal bond had existed, then they would have destroyed it without a qualm since no one, as her uncle had stated, knew of Andrew Gledstane's whereabouts nor when he would return, or even if he would be in the same mind. She was certain that they had falsified Grandfather's will. And doubtless Uncle Wat had already decided upon her future, to be sold as bond-woman into what amounted to slavery. He must have seen Gledstane House with its new owner, Lord Laverock, lacking servants, as a heaven-sent opportunity.

Kirsty would have given much to have been present at his meeting with Dirk Farr. Now denied her birthright, denied even the common humanity of returning to Braehead for her grandfather's funeral, blinded by tears, she watched the solemn procession move slowly down the High Street.

Not only was this to be her last farewell to her grandfather; it was also farewell to her life in Cramond. Existence from this day forward would be a strong and bitter taste of the real world that Grandfather had spared her, for had she truly been his "little princess", a king's daughter, Grandfather could not have treated her more royally, protecting her from every harsh wind that blew. How Aunt Grizel with her loutish snivelling brood must have seethed under such preferential treatment, Kirsty thought, and realised that the woman had hated her for no other reason than that she was the favourite grandchild. Perhaps Aunt Grizel had been plotting such a revenge as this over many years, since her birth. For Grandfather had loved his only daughter and not his only surviving son.

Was it true, Kirsty wondered, the rumour that she had overheard in the Ainslie Tavern? Could such a thing be possible? She recalled the oft-repeated tale of the housekeeper at Braehead, of how Grandfather Howison had rescued the Queen's father from brigands and how King Jamie had become a constant visitor, stretching out his long legs before the kitchen fire.

Kirsty remembered having asked: "Would that be when my dear mother was alive?" And how in answer, a shadow secret and swift had clouded Mistress Booth's face. "Aye, 'twas about that time."

"Before my poor father drowned?" Kirsty had continued innocently.

"Afore that." And Mistress Booth, clearing her throat, had puffed plumply to her feet, suddenly busy about nothing in particular. It now occurred to Kirsty that this scene between them on the matter of the late King's visits to Braehead always ended with Mistress Booth's agitated, guilty manner, as if she felt she had said too much.

Kirsty had never fared any better with Grandfather either. Close-questioned on the matter of her late parents, he would invariably remember some pressing appointment elsewhere. As to the kind respectful devotion of the servants at Braehead, she had accepted that as a matter of course, like the sad but inescapable fact of being parentless, although being an orphan was not in the least remarkable, since death stalked town and village alike, regularly scything down entire families in outbreaks of cholera and pestilence; to which had been added recently another fever of French origin, known as "the new Influence".

As the procession disappeared from view, the weather too mocked Kirsty's grief. The day and her sorrow demanded sad rain to fall, bitter tempest and a mourning sky, not this blithe bonny day of drowsy sunlight, of cheerful eager, birdsong and the sheep bleating in the pastures close by.

She looked at the mourning gown which convention demanded, its black velvet shabby and threadbare in the sunshine. She hated it for carrying the stale body-smell of Aunt Grizel and the ghosts of other mourners who had worn it. She could not imagine her aunt in tears about anything but angry frustration at not getting her own way for her own selfish demands.

Drying her tears, she decided to go indoors and await her release from the locked parlour, when a faint cheering arose from the direction in which the Braehead procession had departed. Curiously, she watched and listened. The sound of horses, of eager and excited voices, of footsteps as people darted from houses and raced across the cobblestones.

"The Queen – the Queen comes!"

A cavalcade, with uniforms and gowns bright as a rainbow, trotted up the street. Curiosity made her lean over the balcony. Curiosity also led the four maids-of-honour of the Queen, her Maries, to glance in the direction of Kirsty Howison. Like their Royal mistress she wore deep mourning. The Queen's black velvet bongrace fell from her white hood, and Kirsty's plain white coif hid her blonde hair. Both wore white sleeves to their gowns, the only – and very vital – difference was that Kirsty's gown was old-fashioned, shabby and unadorned, while the Queen's gown, white-ruffed, sparkled with pearls and jewels.

Kirsty was aware that her presence had drawn comment from the royal party. One of the Maries pointed to the balcony and whispered to her companion, who looked in Kirsty's direction, and then, wide-eyed, whispered to another of the maids. She saw curious glance become bewilderment as the fourth Marie moved forward and touched the Queen's sleeve. The Queen now reined in her horse and also stared up at Kirsty before exchanging some smiling comment with her maids. All of them laughed somewhat dutifully, thought Kirsty, then with a small Gallic shrug of the shoulders, the Queen dismissed the incident and rode on.

Kirsty's attention had been concentrated upon the mysterious behaviour of the four Maries, and so held by the Queen's dazzling appearance that she failed to notice the remainder of the cavalcade which consisted of the *Garde Ecossaise*. Splendid in black velvet and silver cloaks with cuirasses embossed with the *fleur-de-lys*, sashed in red tartan, the sun gleaming on red-plumed steel bonnets, they rode proud and close to their Queen. As they reached Gledstane House, one man, the leader, saluted his comrades as a soldier formally relieved of guard duty.

And Kirsty saw the dark face of Dirk Farr staring up at her. She moved hastily from the balcony, but by the time she had reached the locked door it seemed that he was already turning the key. Escape was the only idea in her mind at that moment, and she hastened to slip past him. However, he took a firm grip on her arms.

"Allow me to leave, sir. I beg of you – I will not be restrained thus."

His hands were not ungentle, nor was his voice. "Before you leave, it is best that we talk together, for there is much you must try to understand."

"I have naught to say to you, sir, except that your behaviour towards me is despicable. No decent lass could accept gladly such a proposition."

Closing the door, he leaned against it and put down the steel bonnet and his cloak upon the small table. Unfastening the cuirass as if its weight burdened him, this too with the tartan sash he laid aside and stood before her in white doublet, leather breeks and thigh-boots.

"You know naught of my proposition – of my conduct – yet," he replied mockingly. There was a hint of the threat of things to come, she felt uneasily, embarrassed too, as he proceeded to unlace the points of his sleeves as he spoke, his eyes never leaving her face.

Laying aside the ceremonial ruff, with its silver facings, he sighed. "That is better. Now we can be comfortable and talk together. Come, mistress, Eunice will bring us wine and food. Come," he said again, taking her arm, and she solidly planted both feet together upon the floor. Suddenly he laughed at her solemnity.

"Mistress, mistress, you have the look of a wildcat about to spring at my throat and before God I am weary and in no mood for sharp claws."

Eunice entered with a tray, grumbling under her breath, although her curtsey to Dirk Farr was neat enough not to cause comment. Still holding Kirsty's arm, Dirk led her to a chair by the fire.

"There now, sit down – and be patient with me." She looked longingly towards the plate with its roast fowl, which she suspected might be tough with Eunice's cooking, although it smelt delicious, and she was hungry.

Dirk Farr interpreted her need and handing her a linen napkin, a plate and a piece of the meat with a chunk of rather coarse bread, he said: "Eat now."

Gladly she did so, while he continued: "I presume by your unfriendly manner that your uncle told you of my intent." He laughed. "And I see that it found little favour with you. As I suspected." He sighed. "A pity, since I flattered myself that you might be happy to live at Gledstane House in Edinburgh rather than at Braehead in Cramond at the mercy of your uncle and aunt. After all, you know this house well. Does Edinburgh not appeal to you?"

"It does, sir, but only with a husband of my own choosing."

"For the moment we talk only of servants, not of husbands. Let us begin at the beginning. Your uncle wished me to buy you as bond-woman into service in this house, or wherever I should wish to send you. He was eager to complete this transaction before leaving Edinburgh, and his manner would brook no delay, no indecision."

And Kirsty knew that much was true.

"He has no love for you, mistress. Concerning his guardianship of your person, he regards you but as a commodity to sell to the highest bidder – and whether into marriage or serfdom is one and the same to him."

"You tell me what I already know."

She thought she saw compassion in his eyes. "I did not see you as servant in this house, for my Romanies would resent a Gorgio and I am in honour bound not to take the bread out of their mouths by providing for others than my Farrs. Besides, I would not wish to have Gorgio servants, since Romanies are a great deal more honest and trustworthy."

"Sir, I do not see what this talk of Romanies has to do with handfasting – the trial marriage, which my uncle said he had arranged."

He looked at her as if weighing his words carefully. "To put it plain, I do not lack servants but I do lack a wife. And with some urgency, since I am concerned with my inheritance at Laverock. I will not weary you with details, but there are others of the Laverock family who contest my rights, claiming that my mother was not legally married to my father since they were not married in the Kirk, but first under gipsy law and then by Scottish tradition of declaring themselves husband and wife before witnesses. My mother is distressed by these new events, and urges me to take a wife and to establish my claim firmly with an heir, since my rival is an elderly man, a widower and childless." He sighed. "I have little time to court a wife."

"I should have thought there were pretty maids in plenty at Holyrood, eager and willing to be Lady Laverock," Kirsty flashed.

He smiled. "My mother wishes me to wed a Romany girl, a cousin. We were childhood sweethearts, but I wish to choose other than my wild gipsy bride, since I do not feel she has the attributes of the future mistress of Laverock. There is a further complication. She has a younger sister, and under Romany law, it would be expected of me to wed both girls rather than show preference for one, since they are orphaned and have only one brother. You look surprised."

"You are allowed two wives?"

"Aye, more than that. There is nothing immoral in such marriages, since it is common practice in small societies where men lead uncertain lives and die young, that the line shall continue by their children being many." He laughed and shook his head. "I see such reasoning is quite beyond you, so let us say instead that I am eager to comply with the customs of the house I have inherited, the house of Laverock, and strengthen my position there with an acceptable Gorgio bride."

Kirsty straightened her back rigidly against the chair. "Then I must say again, sir, that you do me too much honour. There are many others, non-Romanies, who would serve your needs better than myself."

Again he shook his head. "Not in this instance. The matter is urgent. There are none I would wish to court, or have the time to search out in the free hours Her Majesty the Queen leaves at my disposal."

"You are monstrous cold-blooded, sir."

"That I am not, I assure you." And his eyes were suddenly warm, laughing at her blushes. "As you are aware, it is enough under Scottish law for us to be handfasted for a year and a day, a suitable courtship time for us to decide whether we wish, at the end of it, to continue on to a more permanent relationship. My gipsy cousins will be resigned; women have few rights and little say in men's affairs, unless they are as powerful as my mother, who is a queen of the Farr clan in her own right. Aye, honour will be satisfied."

"Yours, perhaps, but not mine!"

He made a wry face. "I am no more eager than yourself to be tied to a cold wife and a loveless marriage. I treasure greatly my freedom and I cannot say, although you are bonny enough, that I am mad for love of you – or likely to be so—"

"Then why?"

"I cannot lie to my mother or to the Farrs. It is sufficient for them – and for the Laverocks – to know that I am handfasted, that I have chosen a wife. A wife," he looked at her steadily, appraising her slowly in the same way that he would have chosen a horse, "with breeding, education and with an intriguing history." Now he studied her face intently. "I expect that others have told you that you are the Queen's image?"

"A silly coincidence, one that interests me little," she said scornfully.

"Does it indeed? Then I can assure you that once you are established in Edinburgh many other people than myself are going to find your likeness to the Queen a fascinating topic for gossip."

"Gossip?"

"Aye, mistress. And now we come to the nub of the story, the reason why I regarded your uncle's offer as a piece of unexpected good fortune. It is common knowledge that the Queen's late father was a lover of women, who fathered a considerable number of bastards, some of whom he claimed, others he ignored. The story of your grandfather, Jock Howison's rescue of King Jamie and the reward of the lands of Braehead he received, is also well known." He stopped and jabbed a finger towards her. "But I had only to take one look at you when we first met, and then to learn the name of the old man I found dying on my doorstep, and from whence you both came, to know the truth. I returned to Holyrood and long before I saw the Queen walking along the corridor, I realised you were her image. You are, Kirsty Howison, without the least doubt in my mind, King Jamie's daughter."

"You cannot prove it. It is a mere rumour, knowing the king's reputation."

"And in common with most rumours, built upon a grain of truth. Anyone who talks to the Queen as I talk to you now, must be struck immediately by the likeness. True, she is tall and you are short, your hair is fair and straight, hers is more red and wavy, but sit you down, cover your hair, and you could be sisters. And I am certain, that you are both the king's daughters." He regarded her with satisfaction. "You no longer scowl. Do you believe me?"

Kirsty felt her heart hammering. Could it indeed be true? She remembered the servants' whispers at Braehead, stifled by her sudden appearance, Mistress Booth's secret expression, the Ainslie's conversation overheard in which they discussed her likeness to the Queen. And most of all her grandfather's dying words, calling her his "little princess" and whispering: "You are truly a king's daughter."

Dirk Farr took her silence for assent. "As you know, I am devoted to Her Majesty. I would gladly die for her – and perhaps I shall have to some day. As a commoner, I would have little chance of a Royal half-sister in marriage. As a gipsy, I am acquisitive, conscious that marriage with such a one as yourself brings me prestige as well as gratification."

"You are scarcely modest, sir."

"But honest, you must allow me that," he responded. "But we digress. I cared not for the idea of my Queen's unacknowledged half-sister ending as a sleazy kitchen slave or a tavern wench, which you should know was your uncle's intent. Now what say you, mistress? Will you stay here with me at Gledstane House and let us get to know one another better? I make no demands upon your person – unless," he added with a mocking smile, "unless we are both of a mind."

Kirsty knew she was defeated, trapped too. If she fled

from him, where could she go, where could she find someone to hide her? The law, cruel as it was, was on the side of men like Walter Howison and Dirk Farr.

"I shall treat you as a guardian would his ward; better, I fancy, than the treatment you would have received from your uncle," Dirk Farr continued. "If, at the end of a year, we have become attached to one another we shall marry, but if we have no wish to do so, upon closer acquaintance, then I shall settle upon you a large sum of money, enough to encourage a rich – and I trust devoted – husband."

Kirsty shook her head. His suggestion was audacious, that she should be traded like merchandise if she failed to please him.

"Come now," he said, "am I such an ogre? Surely 'tis better to be my ward – and perhaps eventually my mistress," he added softly, "than a kitchen slave."

"There is one matter of which you know nothing, a matter which my uncle chose to ignore," she blurted out.

Dirk poured more wine into her goblet. "And what is that?"

"I am, sir, betrothed already." If she expected the statement to enrage or surprise him as the shattering of his hopes, then she was disappointed.

"May I know the fortunate gentleman's name?" His voice was cold as his eyes, the only sign that her information had disturbed him.

"Andrew Gledstane, sir, son of this house."

Dirk Farr laughed softly. "Then, mistress, I have news that will put your mind at rest over breaking your vow to Master Gledstane." He went to a chest by the wall and withdrew some documents. "Ah, here it is. Read it, mistress, the very reason for Master Gledstane wishing to sell this house."

Kirsty took the document from him. To see her beloved Andrew's handwriting again! She longed to press it to her lips. But as she read on, first with incredulity then with bitter tear-filled eyes, she learned the truth of Andrew's failure to communicate with her.

He did not intend to return to Edinburgh and was most

willing to sell his house to Lord Laverock, since in the Hague he had met a lady, a wealthy merchant's daughter, who had family ties and wished to remain in the vicinity.

Gently Dirk Farr took the paper from her. "You need have no qualms, then, over Master Gledstane. I imagine that he is by now happily wed to his Dutch lady."

CHAPTER
FIVE

FOR Kirsty, who had endured so much, the letter from
Andrew was the final defeat. She had suffered her grandfather's death, her uncle's vile abuse, his iniquitous bond to
tear her from Braehead for ever, Dirk Farr's mockery, and
now the one hope which had supported her, that Andrew
loved her and would in good time return to claim her, was
severed.

Broken, defenceless, she bit her lips against the tears
which threatened. She would not show this heartless man her
agony. But he seemed to understand, for his voice was unex-
pectedly gentle.

"You must rest – Eunice has prepared a bedchamber for
you."

"Thank you, sir. I would prefer to return to the Ainslies,
who will be anxious about me."

He shook his head. "The Ainslies have been informed that
you are remaining in this house meantime. They know
nothing yet of your uncle's departure to Cramond."

"Then you lied to them!"

"With reason, mistress." He sighed. "You must decide
how you are to be treated in my house – as a servant or
mistress. Come," he added and she followed him upstairs
where he opened the door of the chamber she had occupied in
happier days. She wondered if he had known that already.

Was he in truth a warlock? she thought, glancing nervously at the cats who slunk alongside, mewing at their progress, but keeping a safe distance. As if he read her thought, he
smiled.

"Do not fear, mistress, I will not make any bodily claims
upon you until you are ready to receive them. Reluctant

brides are not to my taste, when there are wenches in plenty ready and willing enough at Holyroodhouse, for an hour's entertainment. I would rather we took time to know one another, before we go further." He smiled. "Perhaps you might come to regard me with less distaste than at this moment."

She glared at him, her fists clenched. "I think that is most unlikely, sir, since you invite me to be honest. I have no wish to belong to you either as servant or betrothed, each is equally hateful."

He shrugged. "The choice is yours. Are you then to live in the kitchen under Eunice's orders and any of the Romanies whom I choose to bring? I assure you they will regard you with mistrust as a Gorgio. With many old scores to settle they will not be kind to you, and you will constantly be under surveillance as a disloyal and rebellious hireling. I assure you the other choice is more comfortable. If Eunice and my Romanies understand that you are my prospective bride, then you will have respect – and freedom – as the mistress of Gledstane House. My Romanies are romantic despite their barbaric appearance, and the pretext that we love one another will appeal to them."

The one word in his long speech which stood out from all the other arguments was the magic word "freedom". By accepting his proposition, she would be free. She might even escape.

"It shall be as you wish," she said.

For a moment he frowned at this unexpected docility, as if he suspected her downcast eyes held deceit. Seizing her chin, he forced her to face him, and as if satisfied, said: "Here is my hand – and yours – the bargain is sealed." His hands were warm and strong. "I will find you a personal maid. One of your own people from Holyrood, I imagine that would be more to your taste than a Romany maid." When she nodded assent, he continued: "I return to Holyrood within the hour. Eunice will bring food and wine when you request it."

"Tell her I want nothing. I wish to rest."

He bowed. The door closed gently and she was alone. She

looked around the bedchamber, still as she remembered it. The bed was luxuriously feather-mattressed and down-pillowed, covered in finest holland with soft fustian blankets for additional warmth. A fire burned in the grate, for although it was late spring, the window faced to the north-east and the room escaped the sun except in the morning. She touched the elegant damask bed-curtains, silk embroidered with gold tassels. How charming she had always thought this, her lodging in Edinburgh, a contrast to Braehead which lacked the fashionable luxuries that Master Gledstane had been able to afford. In this house, even bedchambers posses-sed the new padded chairs, and only the servants dined on wooden benches.

The bed awaited her, tempting, inviting. Suddenly Kirsty was glad to be alone and although she believed her troubles were great enough to keep her from sleep, she closed her eyes to awake to the light of early evening. Dusk gathered in the chamber beyond the bed-curtains, and putting on her gown, she crept downstairs.

In the kitchen, old Eunice snored and besides the cats who had gathered in a silent circle around the fireplace, yearning for the extra warmth of a dying fire, and who now regarded her balefully, there was a basket in one corner containing newcomers. She discovered two puppies who whimpered, shivered, and weakly wagged their tails as she approached. Although they were small, perhaps a few weeks old, they were unmistakably younger versions of the great hound who accompanied Dirk Farr on his travels. At one time Kirsty would have paused to greet them, for she found young ani-mals irresistible. However, she found the kitchen door into the garden unlocked and by running across the orchard and keeping to the lane where none would see her, five minutes later she was in the Ainslie Tavern pouring out her heart to Rose, whose task it was to supervise the bedding of her young brothers.

Breathlessly, tearfully, Kirsty came to the end of her sorry tale of abandonment and duplicity. Rose listened wide-eyed and for once, could think of nothing helpful and murmured constantly: "I cannot believe it, Kirsty – I cannot believe that all this has happened to you in so short a time. Your grandfather gone – Andrew gone – your vile uncle selling you – and now handfasted to Lord Laverock!"

Mistress Ainslie entered and the story was retold.

"Can you believe it, Mam," said Rose, "our poor Kirsty to wed that warlock – if he still wants her – afterwards," she added with a significant look. "Oh, Mam, I beg of you, let her remain here with us. Do not go back, Kirsty – we will keep you," she said putting an arm around her shoulders. "Won't we, Mam? Poor Kirsty!"

"I will do anything, Mistress Ainslie. Anything – no task would be too menial, if you will let me stay here."

Rose's mother looked from one lass to the other and smiled. "You are welcome indeed, Kirsty, for my part. And no servant would you be, for you are more like kin."

"There now, there now," said Rose. "Did I not tell you that Mam would know what to do, that Mam would see you right?"

"A moment, daughter. As I say, Kirsty is right welcome to bide with us – but first you must ask your father."

Master Ainslie was sought and the story poured out while he listened with a bewildered face. At the end, Rose said: "She can bide with us, can she no', Da?"

Her parents exchanged glances and slowly Master Ainslie shook his head. "You know not what you ask, daughter." Then to Kirsty, he said: "Kirsty, lass, we have aye cared for you, you are like kin to us and we had great regard for your grandfather. But you know not what Rose asks. For us to offer sanctuary or shelter, to take you from Lord Laverock, is against the very letter of the law. We would be guilty of abduction, he could take us to the courts and our homes and property would be forfeit. 'Tis worse in my lord's case, for he is a guardian of the Queen's person, and as such is also offered the protection of the Crown."

Mistress Ainslie's eyes widened in horror. "We would not only lose our home, everything we possess but our lives too might be forfeit for sheltering you."

"You are right," said her husband gloomily. "It would be accounted a treasonable offence. The power of the lords, especially those close to the Queen, is absolute." He laughed without mirth. "Small wonder my Lord Laverock is anxious to keep Her Majesty's favour by refusing to take a gipsy bride from Clan Farr. If we have a wrong-doer under our roof, and we succour him and allow him to escape, under the law we can be held responsible for his crimes and be fined—"

"I am no criminal, no wrong-doer," Kirsty interrupted indignantly. "I am Kirsty Howison, more sinned against than sinning. Surely you can all see that?"

They looked at her solemnly. "You are Lord Laverock's property, his servant or his ward until you are wed. And we can do nothing. Any help we give you, then we are guilty of theft under the law."

Mistress Ainslie came forward and took Kirsty in her arms. "We love you, lass. But we have bairns of our own, a braw tavern which is thriving. We have too much to lose. Even if this were our own Rose here in your situation, we could not help her against the Queen's authority."

"I am grateful to you for your love," said Kirsty, "but I would have no one suffer the inside of the Tolbooth on my account. I will return to Gledstane House – and my Lord Laverock."

Even as she said the words, she knew she was trapped, little better than a caged animal, for there was no escape.

"You may stay until curfew, and welcome. You may come whenever you wish, lass, but you cannot remain under this roof without my lord's permission." And giving her daughter last-minute instructions about bedtime preparations for her brothers, Mistress Ainslie returned to the tavern, already busy with its evening trade.

Rose made a face. "I must go, Kirsty. The lads will get out of hand, they always do, if I am not severe with them."

At that moment, the air around them was pierced by strong yells. Rose hurried to the cradle in the corner and took up the babe Tom, one of whose cheeks was bright red.

"None of us slept last night," she said grumpily, "for this wee lad kept us all awake. He has sore gums, his teeth trouble him in the coming."

Another noise filled the air, the unmistakable shrieks of small boys fighting accompanied by a crash, the sound of a breakage.

"Oh, I knew something like this would happen! Mam will have the skin off my back, if it's one of her precious ornaments," said Rose.

"Give Tom to me," said Kirsty, "go you to your brothers." As soon as she picked him up and cradled his hot face to her breast, he gave a happy sigh, although an occasional sob and hiccup racked his tiny body. Kirsty rested one small starfish hand upon her own and thought how sweet and tender must be the feelings of motherhood. Only a little while ago, she had held this babe as now and believed that such was the fate destiny intended for her – when Andrew returned. She bit back tears. Perhaps she would never be a mother, perhaps she would never know the sadness as well as the joy, since of the many children born, few lived beyond their first year. Fortunate indeed were those parents like the Ainslies, who saw even half of their brood survive into childhood, and even then, the old man with the scythe usually had his way with them, carrying them from the field of life long ere adulthood came.

Beyond the candles which Mistress Ainslie had lit, the bright evening sky had darkened as storm-clouds scurried across the sky. Since the coming of Mary Stuart to her kingdom, it had been observed that the weather, the very seasons themselves, had taken a peculiar turn for the worse. Weather was no longer reliable and there were many folk who whispered that this was an omen of the Queen's reign. She had arrived in Scotland accompanied by a storm. There had been none to greet her and she carried the doleful memory of a ship sinking with all hands as she left the shores of France. In Leith, she had had to seek shelter from the rain and ride into Edinburgh upon an old nag, with her fine white horses lost.

And now Kirsty saw that the Queen's weather continued. Carrying wee Tom to the window, she saw the dark clouds sweeping down from the castle like a black and desolate ragged army. A few moments later the clatter of hailstones thudded upon the rooftops. Whether one was superstitious or no, there seemed a particular malevolence about this weather.

There were footsteps on the forestair and the door opened to Master Ainslie, who ushered in two men, already shaking the hail off their cloaks and bonnets. They were young and tall and splendid, courtiers by their handsome garments and undoubtedly from Holyrood, thought Kirsty, amused by the younger one's furtive manner. He clearly did not wish to be recognised, since he kept his face averted, and quickly resumed his bonnet. Pulling it well down over his brow, he endeavoured to remain in the shadows.

"These, good sirs, are our private apartments," said Master Ainslie, "where you may rest and take refreshment away from the common folk." In an aside, he whispered to Kirsty. " 'Tis Lord James, Her Majesty's brother, with a young companion."

The Earl of Moray! Kirsty was impressed indeed by the royal visitor, and rising to her feet she curtseyed, somewhat hampered by wee Tom.

"Nay, mistress, be at peace. We stand not upon ceremony. Fetch us wine, if you please, good Master Ainslie," said the younger gentleman, whose light but pleasant voice had a slight foreign accent.

Deciding that the youth must be French, Kirsty studied the Earl of Moray, dark-bearded and distinguished in appearance. So this was the Queen's half-brother, whom according to rumours which had drifted out even to Cramond, many distrusted, for he was believed to be plotting against Mary and, some said, would have given the world and his immortal soul, to be the legitimate heir to the throne of Scotland. She could see how such whispers arose, for the Earl had a secret face, a withdrawn inward look, tight-locked, an expression humbler folk classed as "streekit".

His young companion was as tall as he, and the face Kirsty glimpsed briefly beneath the bonnet was that of a beardless boy, soft and gently contoured with dark doe-shaped eyes, a small, pouting but perfect mouth. There was also a glimpse of reddish hair which he strove to push out of sight.

Kirsty was very conscious of his eyes as she rocked the babe nodding sleepily in her arms. A growl of thunder reverberated through the room, shaking the handsome tapestries, and wee Tom, jerked out of sleep, began to scream in terror.

"Hush, now, hush," she said, but his face merely reddened to bursting point as he contributed to the noise of the storm. "I beg pardon, sirs." And noticing how Lord James scowled: "I will remove him."

"Stay!" said the soft-faced youth. "He is so afraid, the little one." He smiled and as Kirsty, embarrassed by the screaming child, tried in vain to quiet him, the youth stretched out his hands; "*Le pauvre petit,* give him to me."

"Nay –" began Lord James warningly, but the youth sprang lightly to his feet and stretched out firm but elegant hands for the crying infant, who, surprised and overwhelmed by the sudden predominance of silks and satins worn by his new companion, began to crow with delight at the bauble – a gold chain richly jewelled – shaken for his delight.

"Go, wench, see what has overtaken our order for wine," commanded Lord James, frowning. Kirsty did as she was told, meeting Mistress Ainslie on the stairs and taking the tray from her. Back inside the parlour, she surprised a look of wistful yearning on the youth's face as wee Tom demonstrated his most captivating gurgles and toothless smiles for the visitor's delight.

Lord James seized his wine, remarkably unmoved by this domestic scene.

The door opened to admit two girls who immediately curtseyed before the couple. Kirsty recognised the newcomers as maids of honour, whom she had seen riding up the High Street at the Queen's side.

"Your Majesty – my lord —"

"We apologise for losing you," said the other.

" 'Twas with some difficulty we found Your Majesty," said her companion reproachfully, while Kirsty wondered at the strange manner of address. Surely they would not call Lord James Stuart "Your Majesty", or was such the proper address for a Queen's half-brother?

The youth gave a delighted chuckle. "Be calm, Livingstone – and you too, Beaton, you are like a couple of mother hens," he added as Mary Beaton seized wee Tom and thrust him rather angrily back into Kirsty's arms. At that moment, the doorway was frame to a red-plumed steel bonnet and the black and silver of one of the Queen's guards.

With an inward groan, Kirsty watched Dirk Farr stride into the room.

"Your Majesty," he said, bowing low to the youth, "God be thanked that you are safe. Your maids were fearful—"

The youth shook his head, smiling. "My maids are over-fanciful. But there was no need for fears, my lord, since my good brother here takes good care of me."

Both the Maries began to talk at once and Lord James held up his hand. "Be silent, both of you." Then to Kirsty he said: "We trust your discretion, mistress, not to spread the rumour of Her Majesty's visit."

"What nonsense is this, brother? All of Edinburgh is aware that their Queen goes out in the evening and mingles with her subjects, wearing boy's apparel," said the youth, laughing.

Lord James winced. "I repeat – this must go no further, since Her Majesty's reputation would be ill-used by such behaviour becoming common knowledge."

"Queens make behaviour and reputations, good brother, may I remind you," the youth said gently. Then, with a laugh, he pulled off the boy's bonnet and shook free a cloud of auburn hair. "Gently, James, gently, you make the lass afraid, and in truth 'tis not her fault, for the indiscretion is ours." Her smile at Kirsty, besides being reassuring and pleasant, was also the smile exchanged between women with a secret. It bound Kirsty to her in the role of confidante.

She was aware that the two Maries were staring at her. They exchanged glances, and the one addressed as Livingstone moved forward and spoke in a low voice to the Queen. Now it was the Queen's turn to stare in her direction. Then, smiling, she came forward and looked intently into Kirsty's face.

"What is your name, mistress?"

"Kirsty Howison, Your Majesty," she said, curtseying.

"Howison – from Cramond?"

"Aye, Your Majesty."

"Is Jock Howison kin to you?"

"My grandfather, Your Majesty – now alas, dead."

The Queen no longer smiled. "I might have guessed that you were related. What do you here – for when last we saw you, you were at Gledstane House. Are you a servant?"

"Nay, Your Majesty. I – I live at Gledstane House." Kirsty darted an appealing look in Dirk Farr's direction, for he had remained silent.

The Queen took in Kirsty's shabby gown. "You are servant there?"

Dirk Farr bowed and came to Kirsty's side. "Nay, Your Majesty. Kirsty Howison is my betrothed."

The Queen surveyed them, hands on hips. "Is she indeed, my Lord Laverock? This event is somewhat sudden."

"It is, Your Majesty. As recent as her grandfather's death."

The Queen frowned. "It is usual, my lord, for those who are my bodyguards to request my pleasure in matters regarding changes of estate, such as matrimony." Her tone was a reproof, and Dirk Farr had the grace to look embarrassed.

" 'Tis not so binding as marriage yet, Your Majesty. We are but handfasted."

"We will talk of this later, my Lord Laverock." The Queen's voice was ice-cold.

"Madam," said Lord James from the window, "it appears that the storm has ceased for the moment. Perhaps we should venture to leave now, before any further misfortune befalls us."

"Your guards await you below, Your Majesty," said Dirk Farr bowing, as Lord James seized the cloak that the Queen had worn and thrust it about her shoulders.

"My cloak, Laverock," he said, pointing to the garment which lay nearby. Dirk Farr picked it up and draped it around Lord James, his manner humble. And Kirsty hid a smile, for Lord James' manner was infinitely more regal than the Queen's and he behaved in the manner of one who refused to do anything for himself, if there were a lesser mortal in sight.

The Queen stretched out long tapering fingers for Kirsty to kiss. "We may meet again, Mistress Howison, if like attracts like." Her smile was gracious and in that moment, Kirsty understood something of her charisma. Here was a Queen who was also a woman, who would treat all her subjects to the same charm and gentleness, making the poorest at ease in her presence.

Following the royal party to the door, Dirk Farr said to Kirsty: "You will remain here until I return for you."

"There is no need. I will make my own way back to your house, sir."

"You will do as I say. It is almost curfew and since there has been a riot among the apprentices and a man slain, the curfew is being observed most strictly. Which is why there was alarm for the Queen's safety, and any who are taken on the streets will be thrown into the Tolbooth."

Neither Rose nor her parents were greatly surprised or impressed when curiosity about the party leaving under guard had them speeding upstairs.

"The Queen herself – disguised as a boy," said Kirsty excitedly.

Master Ainslie nodded. "I thought 'twas no boy," he said, wise after the event. "Like her late father the King, she enjoys naught better than stravaiguing about the town, talking to the citizens in their humble abodes, disguised as a traveller."

"Aye, and she loves wearing a lad's clothes," said Mistress Ainslie, "which suit her well, since she is so tall. Although it does give Master Knox another cause to roll his eyes and rail at her from the pulpit, for showing off her fine legs."

Kirsty decided that after their evening encounter she would have difficulty in imagining this particular Queen sitting on a throne, wearing a crown and ruling over anyone. Remembering her holding wee Tom so tenderly, she hoped that God would be good and send her a son of her own, and a husband to love her dearly.

Rose made a face at the gloomy sky. "Master Knox blames the Queen for our weather too, the worst in living memory, and says it is a judgement on us for allowing the Mass to be said in Edinburgh. But no one cares, for whenever the Queen goes she carries her own sunshine, the brightness of summer is ever with her. For she loves the common folk and none can depress her spirits for long."

" 'Tis true," said her father approvingly. "And the court at Holyroodhouse is good for business too, with everything worthwhile in Scotland happening on our own doorstep, so to speak."

Dirk Farr appeared at the door and exchanged some civilities with the Ainslies, during which time Rose and her mother eyed him fearfully, and Kirsty could see they were wondering if he was truly a warlock. Master Ainslie's manner was respectful but not excessively so as he was used to the quality's patronage, and one lord was much as another.

At last Dirk turned to Kirsty. "Come now, we must return. It is past curfew, and only my steel bonnet and the *fleur-de-lys* will save us from a cold damp night inside the Tolbooth."

"Take the back way, my lord, through the garden and down the lane. 'Tis quicker and you will reach home without encountering even the curious."

Dirk Farr grinned. "You speak wisely, Master Ainslie. Come, Kirsty."

Kirsty felt they were the object of three fascinated pairs of eyes as they stole out into the night, and she would have given much to have listened to the conversation they left behind.

As they reached the orchard of Gledstane House, Dirk Farr spoke for the first time. She had remained silent, expecting reproaches, anger at her for leaving the house. Now he merely smiled and held out his hand to help her across the ditch.

"Come – I will not eat you. And now we are safe home." As they walked towards the door, he ran a hand gently down her arm, a gesture of reassurance which failed, since it had the opposite effect from the one he intended. To be alone with this man was unthinkable to her. As they walked through the kitchen and upstairs, she heard voices from the parlour. Male voices, with a great deal of laughter.

"My comrades await me. Go you to bed. Go," he said, and as she hesitated he pushed her gently but firmly towards the upper flight of stairs. "We will talk tomorrow morning of your adventures."

In the handsome curtained bed, sleep would not come. Kirsty thought of the Queen, reliving the little scene over and over. From downstairs, sounds of laughter and singing pierced the darkness. Finally, knowing that sleep would not be courted, she decided to slip down to the kitchen and find bread and cheese, and perhaps some milk. The more she thought about it, the hungrier and thirstier she became, for she had eaten little that day.

Creeping past the door from which issued the sounds of good company, of singing and laughter, she also heard the rattle of dice, silence and then cheering, as a winner was declared. A chair scraped across the floor.

"If I win, you shall give her to me, Dirk."

"Nay," said another strange voice. "Not so fast, she is mine—"

"Not yet." The voice was Dirk Farr's.

"It is your turn, Dirk." She heard the rattle of dice. "And if you win then she shall be yours."

"She is mine already, Luke," came Farr's slurred voice. "Since she is legally my property."

"Traitor! You promised—"

Kirsty waited to hear no more. From Dirk Farr's voice, he

was undoubtedly only a little more sober than his comrades. She knew exactly what was happening within the chamber. *They were throwing dice for her!*

Terrified, sickened, she knew she must escape. She ran downstairs into the kitchen. The door was locked. Frantically she turned the heavy key and at that moment, a familiar voice was like a bucket of cold water across her shoulders.

"And where do you go to, my pretty maid?" asked Dirk Farr. Without waiting for answer he took a step forward, seized her arm. Towering over her, she saw that the gentleness of his words was belied by the sheer ferocity of his wolf-like expression, his bared teeth.

She screamed and thrust both hands at his chest. Surprised by her action, he staggered drunkenly, and taking advantage of the moment, she opened the door. He sprang back at her and she tried to drag the door closed in his face.

But he was strong, her small strength availed nothing against him. She was dragged back, picked up bodily and screaming, kicking, she was carried upstairs, to a chorus of amusement from his comrades. They had been alerted by her cries and now their grinning faces delightedly watched their leader's progress as they roared obscene encouragement. They stumbled drunkenly after him up the stairs and he kicked the bedchamber door shut, ignoring their thundering upon the panels. Setting her on her feet, he turned the key and then, seizing her like a sack of barley, he threw her down upon the bed. Holding her flailing arms with one hand about her wrist, his face descended and his mouth covered hers. She fought to be free, her sharp teeth bit into his lip and with a curse he released her.

"Rape," she screamed, "rape!" It was the ancient cry for help, the instinct of many women at many times in history, and like her predecessors, it availed her nothing.

Again he seized her. She moaned and tried to turn from him.

"Rape is what you deserve, my pretty maid."

There was no amusement in his voice now, and again she cried out, expecting the thrust of his body on her. Her mouth was free and she stared into his face, devil-dark with its pale shimmering eyes.

"You promised," she gasped. "You promised. Is this how a Romany keeps his word?"

"I promised nothing. But you did. You promised not to run away, and no sooner was my back turned than you went away to the Ainslies. And now I find you at the dead of night creeping out of my kitchen door. Twice within hours you have broken your promise. Why should I keep mine?"

"Whatever you and your vile comrades do to me you cannot make me stay. I hate you – I hate you!"

He put his hand to his mouth and looked at the blood on it. She saw his lip swollen where her teeth had penetrated. Suddenly he laughed.

"To think that I scorned my mother's wild gipsy brides for a creature like you! Cold and dishonest as well."

She struggled to sit up, expecting to have to fight him off, resolving that she would defend herself to the last ounce of her strength, with little idea what that would avail her against his powerful body. At least she would never submit willingly. He would have no joy of her.

But his hands no longer touched her. He leaned over and gently pulled her to her feet. She was conscious of her lack of inches, her insubstantial frailty, her absurd notion that she could fight this man who could have broken her easily as a Venetian glass goblet shattered upon a stone floor. Yet for all his height, she remembered that he had undeniable grace too. And gentle hands, as he moved the hair back from her forehead, stroked her cheeks dry of tears.

"Why do we quarrel, Kirsty? Am I never to have peace in my own house?"

"Let me go, and then you will have all the peace you want."

He looked at her and shook his head. "What have I done to you? I understand you not, for I thought we made a bargain."

"A bargain, when you and your vile soldiers would dice for me! Is that how you keep your promises?"

"Dice for you? What is this you talk of?"

"Do not deny it. I heard you and your noble *Garde Ecossaise*. I heard you promising your friends that the winner would have – have me – first."

"Have *you* first? Have you taken leave of your senses?"

"I heard you, so you cannot deny your intent, my lord. You told them that you had first right, seeing that I was legally your property. Is that the way you honour bargains?"

Suddenly he began to shake with laughter. Seizing her arm, he propelled her towards the door.

"Let me go – I will not be given to your vile friends!"

"Come with me. Come," he commanded, "or be carried. There is something you must see."

"Never – never!"

"Very well. Do I thrust you into their chamber, let them have their way with you – first come, first served – or do you accompany me downstairs?" He laughed again at her horrified expression. "The devil you know, Kirsty," he whispered, "I assure you is the better choice."

The devil she knew! It was true, just as Rose had told her. This man was a warlock. There was no vileness of which he was incapable. As they reached the chamber where the soldiers' voices filtered through, with the sounds of thrown dice and shouts of laughter, Dirk Farr put a warning finger to his lips.

"Quietly now. Let us not disappoint them, for they imagine their Captain to be engaged on more romantic matters for some time."

"Where are you taking me?"

"Here!" And he thrust open the kitchen door.

"Where is your servant?"

"I gave her leave to return to my Farrs, with a message."

Kirsty groaned. Not even the presence of the servant, vile as the old woman was, to protect her from Dirk Farr's attentions!

Seizing her arm firmly, for she would have fled back upstairs, he marched her over to the basket where the two puppies she had seen earlier now rolled in a sleepy ball of fur.

Stooping down, gently he extracted one. It whimpered in his arms, shivering.

"There, my beauty, there now." Stroking its head, he smiled at Kirsty. "This – this pretty bitch – is the wager we dice for. I brought her from the palace earlier this day. Her sire is the Queen's wolfhound, whom you have encountered already. I intend to keep her brother here," he said, indicating the other pup. "Back you go, my pretty."

Replacing the pup, he stood up and regarded Kirsty with eyes suddenly defeated. Sighing, he stretched his arms above his head. "At last, you have almost convinced me that we can never – could never – have any peaceful life together. Tomorrow I shall make other plans for your future." His face was grim. "And now, will you please retire to your bedchamber and endeavour to restrain your natural desire to spy upon me."

"Spy upon *you*?"

"That is what I said. Your company wearies me and I think I should like to get very drunk. Now go."

As she set foot on the stair, he said: "And please do not bother to lock your door. You would be wasting your time – and mine."

When Kirsty awoke it was almost noon. She had overslept and she was alone in the house. But she did not have long to enjoy the empty kitchen or to wonder how she would spend the day, or what Dirk Farr's plans for her future might be.

She had hardly broken her fast upon indifferent bread, when a messenger arrived. A little later, she was riding behind him, clattering over the drawbridge into the Palace of Holyroodhouse.

She had received a royal summons to attend Her Majesty the Queen that very day.

The Queen's first summons of the day had been to Dirk Farr, who returning to the palace rather the worse for wine imbibed with his comrades, had been hastened to the Queen's presence. He found her angrily pacing the floor of the audience chamber.

"I have been awaiting your arrival, my Lord Laverock, with some considerable impatience," she said coldly.

Her Majesty addressed him formally only when others were present or when she was angry. And Dirk groaned inwardly as he waited for the storm to break over his head.

"Did our ears deceive us yesterday, or were we to understand that you are betrothed to the Howison girl?"

" 'Tis true, Your Majesty."

"True, is it? Is that all you have to say to your Queen?" She jabbed a long forefinger at him. "You know, of course, my lord, that no member of my personal guard or my household is permitted to marry without my assent?" Pausing she looked at him candidly. "Have you got her with child, my lord? Is that the reason for the haste?"

"Nay, Your Majesty, it is not."

"Then you realise that I could have you thrown into the Tolbooth for the offence – both of you?"

Dirk decided to swallow his pride and tell her the truth, relying upon his sovereign's well-known soft spot for starcrossed lovers. He went back to the beginning, omitting nothing, of his meeting with her crafty guardian and the bargain he had made, to be handfasted for a year, then married, if he still wanted her.

"But I fear," he ended, "she will not remain in Gledstane House without restraint. She is a spirited lass and she will run away, whatever the consequences."

"She loves you not?" The Queen sounded surprised when he shook his head and looked miserable. The Howison lass little realised how many women had lost their heads to her handsome bodyguard. Even she herself, had she not been royal – Hastily, Mary dismissed the thought.

"And you love her?"

"With all my heart, madam. And I wish her to be my wife."

The Queen thought for a moment, remembering that she owed Dirk Farr her life and that he carried an assassin's scar near his heart as a memento of the scuffle with a Huguenot fanatic in Paris.

"Then she shall not run away, she shall come here to Holyrood, to service in the palace, where you may woo her and win her – with my blessing. I shall send for her immediately." As she held out her hand for him to kiss, she smiled. "There is one condition, *mon cher*—"

"Whatever you wish, madam."

"This shall be our little secret."

"Of course, madam."

Dirk smiled too, knowing the Queen loved secrets and intrigues of any kind provided they hurt no one. Such were glorious games to Mary Stuart, for whom life in Scotland was often very dull. Her scheming was innocent, playful as a child's, she wanted only the joy of having those around her happy.

Dirk whistled happily under his breath as he took his place on duty outside the royal apartments. He was by nature a gambler: he had taken a chance and won.

CHAPTER
SIX

KIRSTY'S first reaction to her arrival at the Palace of Holyroodhouse was curiosity rather than excitement. After all, attendance upon the Queen for a mere merchant's grand-daughter clearly indicated a menial position in the royal kitchens. Kirsty Howison was a nobody. She need not assume she would ever meet the Queen in her daily tasks, and yet she suspected that Dirk Farr had been behind the request. Perhaps he had decided that this would allow him to keep an eye upon her, she thought angrily.

Approaching the palace, they were dwarfed into insignificance by the huge building with its crenellated battlements, built by the Queen's father. Dominating the landscape, framed by wild country which reached out towards neat gardens and orchards, it stood dark and defiant beneath a glowering sky. Nearness also brought a formidable impression of menacing towers, despite handsome clear-cut lines and majesty. Joined to the palace, Kirsty glimpsed the roofless, windowless ruin of the Abbey of the Holy Rood, which had been burnt by the English nearly twenty years earlier. Unlike the palace which had suffered a similar fate, it had been left to moulder and decay.

She followed the messenger through a cobbled courtyard to the north-west corner where the royal apartments were situated. The kitchen proclaimed its presence by cheerful sounds of voices and the lazy pre-disjune smells of baking meats and pastries.

Each corridor revealed a magnificence which took Kirsty's breath away. She had imagined Gledstane House as the height of luxury. Now it paled into shabbiness, while Braehead seemed primitive indeed compared to the beauty of the

Queen's apartments. Mary Stuart, she learned later, had established a "Little France" in Holyrood, a tiny corner of Scotland which gave her complete privacy and the ability to live her own life, away from the prying eyes of those who disapproved, in particular the eyes of Master John Knox.

Her round tower was equipped after the French fashion. The forbidding stone walls warmed to glowing colours of sylvan and heroic scenes from Gobelin tapestries and carpets from Turkey, rich in dark crimson and the blue of sapphires, intricately designed. Bedchambers which Kirsty glimpsed were furnished by elaborately carved canopied beds in silver and gold while walls held pictures in heavy gold frames. From corridor windows she saw the dark shadow of the park, gentled by the bridal greens of the budded trees of May, flourishing white blossom above the dark shapes of blackbirds, scurrying across the glades, quarrelling over rivals' invasions with shrill warning cries.

A moment later, Kirsty was walking down a long corridor with a fine heraldic painted ceiling. Beyond its windows lay a quiet walled garden with stone seats and arbours to be enjoyed on less chilly days. She saw, too, that security had not been neglected for elegance. The handsome windows were barred by iron gratings and two armed guards held motionless sentinel over the door leading to the Queen's private apartments.

The guards wore the now familiar uniform of plumed steel bonnet and black and silver cloak, with its *fleur-de-lys*. As one briefly raised his eyes, she found herself face to face with Dirk Farr of Laverock. A sudden warmth of her face, the burning of her lips, warned that her senses still remembered Dirk's kisses at Gledstane House, when she had completely misunderstood the nature of his friends' wager. With embarrassment too great to frame the questions she longed to ask him, and receiving no encouragement from his stern and unyielding expression, she curtseyed brief acknowledgement of his bow.

"This way, mistress." The messenger's hand was on her arm, ushering her into the Queen's audience chamber.

As the door closed behind him, all thought of Dirk Farr vanished in the magnificence of the scene around her. Free to explore, Kirsty observed another heraldic ceiling, a great stone fireplace and windows with padded seats gazing down into the gentle harmony of the Queen's garden. She was disappointed to find it bereft of courtiers or pretty maids, with the stone seats already turning black under a heavy downpour, which had drained all colour from sky and earth alike.

A drift of incense reached her and through a small arched doorway she saw a private chapel, empty and silent behind its carved reredos, awaiting with all in readiness the Queen's daily worship and prayers, the altar with its crucifix and Communion vessels. Very different from the Reformed kirk at Cramond, severe and unadorned, thought Kirsty. She turned away hastily, uncomfortable before the images of saints and the expensive white wax candles which suggested all things that Grandfather Howison – in company with Master Knox – despised, the Roman Church and idolatry.

In the audience chamber was the Queen's library of books, finely bound in leather and gold. Works by Erasmus, Rabelais, and lying open on a table, the poems of Ronsard. In no hurry to meet anyone, Kirsty was happy to take a seat in the window, delighted to absorb the atmosphere of luxury and harmony which she imagined she would never again encounter as a visitor. Only a Queen could live thus, she imagined, even when later the Maries' personal maids assured her that Holyrood was but a hovel after the grandeur of the French Court.

At last the door through which she had entered opened. An elderly man with a rosy honest face, white hair and a somewhat military bearing limped towards her. His boots and riding cape were much travel-stained and his nearer presence brought the smell of sweating horses. His manner was urgent and kneeling before her, he kissed the hem of her gown.

"Nigel Armstrong of Heronby, Your Majesty."

Embarrassed, Kirsty shook her head. "Nay, sir – rise, please rise – a mistake—"

The man frowned, staring at her. "There is no mistake, Your Majesty, I bring news from Elizabeth of England."

"Nay, sir – I tell you—" She was fumbling for an explanation when laughter from the open door had him spinning round, a hand flying to the place at his side where a dagger normally hung, since all arms were to be left outside before one entered the Queen's presence chambers.

And it was Mary of Scotland herself who walked swiftly across the room towards him, while he stared like a man possessed from her to Kirsty and back again. Softly the Queen laughed again. How regal, yet voluptuous she was, thought Kirsty, even her walk is an invitation to drive men to madness.

The Queen was followed by two of the Maries, and Kirsty decided to be patient, that in due course she would recognise them and be able to deliver the four names correctly. They wore dark green velvet hunting costumes while the Queen wore soft grey and carried a falcon hooded upon her wrist. Scenting strangers, the bird mewed, protesting, the bells on her feet jingling.

While Kirsty stood up to curtsey, Nigel Armstrong hurried towards the Queen, his neck bright red with embarrassment as he again dropped on one knee before her.

"Your Majesty—" he began.

Kirsty stood by the door, undecided, awaiting dismissal. But the Maries shook their heads in unison, warning her that she was to remain.

"Nigel Armstrong, Your Majesty. Forgive me," he said looking in Kirsty's direction. "I was confused."

The Queen smiled. "So are we all – confused, Master Armstrong. An understandable mistake. But let us waste no more time, for I long to hear the news you bring from my sister of England. Fleming, take care of Mistress Howison. Come, Master Armstrong."

As the door of the Queen's supper-room closed upon them, the tallest of the Maries, whom the Queen had called Fleming, came forward and indicated that Kirsty follow her up a narrow staircase, situated directly above the Royal apartments. Pointing to a door, Fleming said:

"This is the chamber which is occupied by us – the maids of honour. Our personal maids are – there. And you are to have this chamber." So saying, she opened a small door into a turret room. No larger than a pantry at Braehead, it contained one small plain bed and a press, a tiny fireplace and a window which overlooked the ruined Abbey.

"I trust it is not too small."

"Nay, Mistress Fleming. It will do very well."

Fleming smiled and asked if she had previous experience of royal service. Receiving another negative reply she told Kirsty not to be afraid to seek their advice, especially upon matters of conduct and etiquette.

"I can cook a little," said Kirsty, and when Fleming frowned, she said eagerly, "if you will direct me towards the kitchen. . . ."

"The kitchen?" said Livingstone who had followed them upstairs. The next moment both Maries were exchanging glances, with raised eyebrows.

"Nay," said Fleming, " 'tis not the kitchen you are for, Howison. Come." Descending to the audience chamber, Kirsty observed Nigel Armstrong leaving the supper-room and departing hurriedly, like a man with a mission. The Queen watched him go and then took the hands of her two Maries.

"*Mes petites*," she whispered, "is it not splendid? my sister of England and myself are to meet. She is eager for the meeting and has sent Nigel Armstrong, who is familiar with both sides of the Border, to explore the most suitable place."

In the delighted smiles of Fleming and Livingstone, Kirsty had been forgotten. Whatever news Nigel Armstrong brought with such urgency, it had been anxiously awaited and eagerly received.

Suddenly the Maries remembered Kirsty and Fleming whispered to her royal mistress in French.

The Queen regarded Kirsty with laughter-brimming eyes. "Nay, Howison, you are not for the kitchen. My lord Laverock tells me that you are well educated. How so? Did you attend the dominie at Cramond?"

"Nay, Your Majesty. My grandfather had tutors from Edinburgh sent to teach me."

"Do you speak French?"

"Nay, Your Majesty. Nor any other foreign tongue. For my grandfather believed it was necessary only that I should read and write and do my sums, since other matters were costly. I also know a little history and geography."

The Queen smiled. "And do you write a fair hand?"

Her tutors had been proud of her neat writing.

"There is no need for modesty," laughed the Queen. " 'Tis an achievement rare even in my nobles."

So her grandfather had often told her, proud of his daring in educating a mere lass, since even Scottish gentlewomen were rarely bothered about such trivialities.

The Queen was regarding her thoughtfully, chin on hand. "Master Howison must have thought highly of you indeed, to spend money thus upon you."

"Aye, Your Majesty. He believed that such was a necessity of life and should be for maids as well as for men."

"So too my own father, the late king," said Queen Mary softly. "Those were his very words, so I am told."

And in the short silence, Kirsty wondered if the idea was present in both their minds that the same man had fathered a royal princess and Jock Howison's granddaughter.

"Tell me, Howison, do you sew a fine seam as well as write a fine hand?"

"Aye, Your Majesty." And Kirsty smiled at the question, since all lasses, even the most ignorant, unless they lived in noble houses which employed an army of seamstresses, sewed their own garments and wove the household linen and furnishings from the day when they could first hold a distaff and thread a needle.

"Very well, Howison. Mary – Mistress Fleming, who is *femme de ménage* of the royal household, will attend to you."

Almost immediately the royal housekeeper who ruled the domestics with a firm hand, despite her Madonna-like appearance, had Kirsty set before a torn petticoat, which Her Majesty had put a foot through while dancing. This task performed according to her satisfaction, Kirsty was given a delicate lace ruff to repair and to replace the seed pearls which had become loose.

Both Fleming and Livingstone announced themselves well-pleased by her speed and tiny stitches, especially as the ruff belonged to the latter. Having passed this test successfully, Kirsty now expected to be given a place among the many seamstresses occupied by the constant wear and tear of garments in the court.

No such orders came, and she spent the next three days sewing with the Maries, flattered by their presence but irritated beyond measure that they conducted all conversations in French. True, they treated her politely, but she found there was an insurmountable gulf between them and herself. Even their personal maids, who had been with them in France, obviously thought themselves a little above Kirsty Howison and tended to ape their mistresses. Listening to them chattering in French, sharing private jests and merriment, Kirsty felt painfully excluded, as unobserved and uncared-for as a piece of furniture in their presence.

Even the few glimpses she had of Dirk Farr suggested he was indifferent to her presence, since he made no attempt to speak to her beyond an acknowledgement of her existence with the briefest of bows. His neglect stung her into a passion of resentment and she longed for a confidant, someone whose sympathetic ears would understand an outpouring of her woes. Most of all she longed for a warm female companion, loved and trusted like Rose Ainslie, who must be curious indeed after receiving a brief message – if it had ever reached her – that Kirsty had been summoned to Holyroodhouse. Aye, she longed to pour out her tale, sure of Rose's comfort.

Opportunity came earlier than she had expected, when one morning Fleming announced that Howison would not be required until four of the afternoon.

Eager to make her escape to the Ainslie Tavern, Kirsty found Dirk Farr on duty outside the royal apartments. She had not been thus close to him, alone, since her arrival. She stared at him with a cold and distant reserve to hide her agitation. He was so tall, and her head was only as high as his heart. Angrily, she found her own heart behaving in a very disturbing fashion at Dirk's nearness.

When she tried, avoiding his eyes, to thrust past him, he barred her way.

"Let me pass, if you please, my lord." It was a considerable effort to look up into his face, but she was gratified that her voice sounded calmer than she felt at that moment. It gave no indication of her tumult of emotions.

"Upon what authority, mistress?" he asked sternly.

"I am not required by Her Majesty until this afternoon, so I wish to visit my friend Rose." She bit back hot angry words as to whether her destination was any of his concern. How dared he treat her like – like a common serving wench?

"I have not received orders to permit any to leave. Only Mistress Fleming, who is in charge of you, mistress, can give such authority."

Wearily Kirsty turned from him. "Then I will find her."

Dirk Farr smiled bleakly. "You will have difficulty in so doing, since she left more than an hour past and is not expected back before supper."

At this information, Kirsty swung round to face him, her face flushed with anger. Odious man, he was enjoying her disappointment! She raised her fists, longing to strike him.

Luckily at that moment, Livingstone approached. Hastily Dirk Farr explained and to Kirsty's fury, Livingstone nodded in agreement. "I cannot allow you to leave, Howison, only Fleming can do so."

"I wish only to visit my friend in the High Street!"

Livingstone shook her head. "The Queen's personal servants may only travel from the palace by her royal permission and with an escort. You will know better next time."

As Kirsty watched her depart she said to Dirk Farr, "So I am a prisoner! And I imagine I have you to thank for it." She turned on her heel walked swiftly back into the Queen's apartments.

Hatred welled inside her and angry tears of frustration filled her eyes. A prisoner, and even though she dwelt in a velvet-lined luxurious cage, the invisible bars were still of inflexible iron.

"Mistress Howison – I said good day to you."

She stared up into Nigel Armstrong's face, his delaying hand upon her arm.

"What is this? Tears? Who has done this? Tell me his name and I shall run him through with my sword – when I get it back, that is." Although his manner was teasing, Kirsty saw that he was concerned. She was glad of a friend, especially such a kind, fatherly man and she told him her fears that she was a prisoner, at the Queen's pleasure.

They had reached the audience chamber and he led her to a window seat and sat down beside her, taking her hand in consoling fashion.

"I have never been outside these apartments, except to accompany Fleming and Livingstone for a walk in the garden. And then we had to be challenged by – by the Queen's guard."

His smile of sympathy did not indicate that he knew she referred to Dirk Farr of Laverock.

"I meet none but Fleming and Livingstone, since Seton and Beaton are concerned with the Queen's person and rarely leave her side. Everyone talks French at me, even the Maries' personal maids—"

Nigel Armstrong patted her hand. "Come, Kirsty, you exaggerate. These are the conditions of all royal appointments. Even I myself am challenged upon leaving the apartments and have to produce the Queen's permission to come and go. It is all in the interests of the Queen's safety. If her personal servants were allowed to go freely there might be dangers, intrigues against her royal person, of which you know nothing."

"Am I never to be free again? Am I to remain here sewing – like a nun – and never see the outside world again?"

"I am certain that is not the Queen's intention. You say you have no personal maid, for instance. Very well then, the appointment is not to be of long duration, or you would have been given a maid and not set to share those of the Maries."

Although she did not completely believe him, Kirsty was grateful for his consolation, glad of his friendly countenance. In the days that followed their brief argument about leaving the palace, she discovered that Dirk Farr paid her even less attention than before, if such was possible. All his energies seemed to be centred on guarding the royal apartments. There was no room for any other woman in his life, it seemed, but Mary Stuart. Perhaps she should be glad of that, she decided.

Nigel Armstrong told her about his wife and family in Essex, as far away as the moon, she thought, from Holyrood. Once he apologised for mistaking her for the Queen, whom he had met only once before and briefly.

"I could have sworn you were Her Majesty until she entered and you rose to your feet, and I saw how small you were by comparison. And, of course, your voices are quite different."

Kirsty smiled at his frankness. The Queen with her beautiful cultured voice, with its slight French accent, while she spoke the broad Scots tongue of the Lowlands.

"You do not sound like a Borderer, despite your name."

He smiled. "I am from the English Armstrongs. I met my Queen's secretary on my travels abroad and since then have spent many long years in Her Majesty's service as envoy."

She knew the reason for his presence in Holyrood. That he was concerned with exploring a safe and secret route for Queen Elizabeth to journey to the Borders incognito to meet Mary of Scotland. No one could talk of anything else in the palace, since the entire court was now involved in preparations for their royal mistress's border journey. It was all supposedly secret, but she felt this must be the most widely known confidence in the whole of Scotland.

"What of your Queen?" she asked Nigel Armstrong, who spoke the name of Elizabeth of England with pride and reverence. Occasionally Kirsty overheard Queen Mary's none-too-subtle questions about her rival: "Was she beautiful as men said? Why then, did she not marry, being no longer young?"

Master Armstrong thought before answering. "She has the heart of a man and of a king of England inside the frail body of a woman," he said proudly.

"But what does she look like? Is she as handsome as our Queen?"

He frowned. "She is not beautiful in the accepted sense of the word, and no man looking at her portrait would think her so in the least. But she has a clever woman's ability to appear beautiful in the eyes of men – aye, desirable and unforgettable too. These qualities are more enduring than beauty of face and form which are at the mercy of time. Her mother, Anne Boleyn, had the same quality – and it cost her her head." He sighed. "I was young then, and I well remember that lovely lady. She drove Harry of England mad for love of her, but that all-consuming love did not produce the living son he craved."

He paused for a moment, regarding her solemnly. "Elizabeth of England is older – and I think, a little wiser by her years, than your Queen. You too are young – and lovely. Not many storms have furrowed your brow, not many tempests have drawn lines of bitterness about your eyes. Your face, little Kirsty, is still an untrodden path and you see only what is reflected in your mirror – and the admiration in men's eyes."

"You still have not told me the colour of your Queen's hair and eyes," she reminded him gently.

"She is of the colouring of your Queen, since they are bred from the same stock."

"What of her gowns? Are they as handsome?"

"She has more than two thousand, in every style and fashion."

The idea was beyond Kirsty's imagination since gowns were few and so greatly treasured that they were passed down from one generation to the next. Perhaps Mary Stuart possessed fifty gowns, but Kirsty could hardly boast about that when her rival Elizabeth Tudor possessed two thousand.

"She is not only every inch a woman, she is every inch a ruler," Nigel continued, "which your Queen Mary has yet to prove."

"What mean you by that?" asked Kirsty indignantly. "All her subjects love her."

"True, she is exquisite and lovable, but—" he shook his head, "she has an uneasy balance, she has not yet learned that she must be first a queen, second a woman. Her emotions will, I fear, win one day over her head, a sad day for her realm. Queens are not allowed to let their hearts rule and Queen Elizabeth never lets sentiment intervene. Men, statesmen, knowing that she has this masculine quality, respect and adore her the more for it. Why do you smile?"

"Are they all like yourself?"

"What mean you?"

"Are they all a little in love with her?"

He drew himself up proudly. "I am honoured to include myself among her adorers." He looked out of the window, smiling no longer, as if he yearned to see beyond Arthur's Seat, beyond the great length and breadth of Britain, the palace at Whitehall. "I would die for her gladly." He was strangely still and sad, like one who listens to an unheard voice. "Proudly I would die for her, and one day I may have that honour."

Kirsty suspected that Dirk Farr, similarly questioned, would have expressed the same sentiments about Queen Mary. There seemed to be no place for any other woman than his Queen while he guarded the royal apartments. Kirsty told herself that she should be glad he spent so much time there, instead of prying into her activities, innocent as they were. But her wayward heart refused to believe her. It complained that his neglect wounded and upset her and that she would rather quarrel with him any day, than suffer his indifference.

One day, she walked in the garden with the Maries and their maids. Dirk Farr, who was going off-duty, carried his steel bonnet under one arm and hurried across the grass towards them. The Maries, seeing him approach, gave

Kirsty compassionate glances. "We will leave you with my Lord Laverock," said Fleming.

"You have little time together," agreed Livingstone, smiling.

Dirk Farr watched their retreating figures but chose to ignore their remarks. Gravely he fell into step beside Kirsty, who immediately walked briskly ahead. She would show my lord Laverock than she wanted none of him, that she did not pine for his presence, when he felt in a humour to bestow it upon her.

"How like you to serve our Queen?" he asked idly, accommodating his long stride to her smaller steps.

"Well enough, my lord."

"Is that all you can say to such an honour?" His voice was amused.

"I did not mean to sound ungrateful."

"I should hope not, for—" He paused, his sentence unfinished, staring at nothing.

"For I have you to thank for it?" she suggested coldly.

He nodded. "Only in part. The Queen was intrigued by your likeness to her, and when I told her of the situation between us she suggested that it might be more convenient — that we might prefer to be – near to one another." Watching her cold, tight-lipped face, he continued: "I did not feel inclined to discuss the sorry story of matters between us. The Queen has a romantic heart for lovers."

Kirsty stopped and said: "Kind of you, my lord, kind indeed to consider her heart and feelings, since you have never considered mine."

He looked down into her face. "I thought that by arranging this service for you, I might also make up to you for the grievous things that have happened, for your grandfather's death and your uncle's cruel rejection." His face was warm, his voice soft, his eyes compassionate, and for a moment, Kirsty's resolve melted. She longed to be held and comforted. Even as he stretched out his hand to her, she closed her eyes against the tears that threatened. But when she opened her eyes again, she saw that his hands had dropped to his sides. Her gesture had been misunderstood as one of rejection.

"Obviously, mistress, gratitude did not occur to you." His voice was cold, his face remote which had been so warm moments ago.

"Gratitude?" The mention of gratitude stung her into anger. "All I can see clearly, my lord, is that I have exchanged one kind of prison for another."

"What mean you by that? All who attend the Queen's pleasure have to live here by certain rules."

"Then I like not rules which steal my freedom, which tell of where I shall go and who shall be my friends."

"You are fortunate indeed to be of service to Her Majesty, and your remarks would grieve her gentle spirit. When she came into her kingdom here, she brought sunlight into a gloomy austere land." He paused. "A land which I hated, although it gave me birth. After those long years in France, I had forgotten how cold, how dreary, how loathsome are our nobles, lacking finesse and culture. Why, even my gipsies could teach them better manners and morals."

They had reached the gate and bowing, he opened it for her.

"Can you imagine how delighted I was to find a common lass from Braehead, who was educated? Small wonder Her Majesty wishes to have you at Holyrood."

"Even common lasses from Braehead are free to go where they choose. I am a prisoner."

"But not a very unhappy one, if the sound of your laughter so often mingled with Master Armstrong's is aught to go by."

"So you are jealous, sir? Would that you were as great a gentleman as he." Her laugh was contemptuous and he seized her arm, thrusting it behind her so that their bodies touched. She fancied she could hear the beat of his heart through the leather cuirass.

His hold was inescapable as, turning her chin toward him, he bent his mouth to hers. Dizzily she closed her eyes, waiting and longing for his kiss.

"I trust I have no need for jealousy, since you are my

property." His voice was cold and Kirsty stared into his dark unyielding face. Only seconds ago she had longed for this moment, for his compassionate arms, and now with a few words he had destroyed it, belittling her with cruel thoughtless words to suggest that his only interest was a gipsy laird's avarice. Avarice for possessions and for respectability in the eyes of society to be gained by such a prize as Kirsty Howison, half-sister to the Queen of Scots.

Could he not guess that she was desperately lonely, that she needed warmth and love, all the security and happiness which had been cruelly snatched from her by her grandfather's death? Could he not guess that this palace with all its luxuries for which many might have envied her, was still a prison, albeit of velvet instead of stone?

To suggest that she saw Master Armstrong as any other than a kindly elderly man who had befriended her! To suggest she was infatuated! She stared at him with hate in her eyes, contempt for the lust and anger in his face where all should have been tenderness and love.

She struggled against him. "Let me go – oh, let me go."

There were footsteps, voices, but still he held her, his face inches from her own. Where his lips grazed her cheek as she thrust him aside, her face burned, as if from the passion she glimpsed in those crystal-bright eyes.

"Jealous, Kirsty? You think so?" His smile was ice. "Why should I be jealous when I can take you whenever I want you – with or without the Queen's permission?"

CHAPTER
SEVEN

"WHICH shall we choose, Howison, the violet or the green?"

In the gardens beyond the Queen's apartments, the first pale summer roses spread their delicate fragrance on the air. Despite the passage of time and the establishment of a daily routine, Kirsty still felt mild disbelief that the girl sitting opposite her and asking her opinion on matters of gown, could be the Queen of Scots.

On closer acquaintance, embroidering with Her Majesty, Kirsty saw that the beauty for which she was famed was an illusion, belonging not to individual features but to the luminous quality of a transparent skin, light auburn hair and eyes whose strange colour changed with her varying moods. Mary Stuart also had exquisite inborn grace and a love of music, art, philosophy. These were words infrequently upon the lips of the majority of the Scots nobles at court, doubtless the reason why the Queen tolerated the more outrageously effeminate of her French courtiers, Kirsty decided.

She remained in awe of Her Majesty, who took so little heed of her royalty that she had a word, a jest, for everyone – the highest and the lowest of her subjects. She was also sensitive, longing to please all, Kirsty observed, wanting to live in harmony and hating discord. She lived in abject fear of the cruel tongue of Master John Knox and his vile insinuations. She could weep for a day over an unknown child trampled beneath the hooves of her cavalcade galloping along the High Street. As for that magic appeal which uncharitable folk put down to witchcraft, there were no secret unguents, only the radiance of charm, encompassing all.

"I think the green velvet, madam." Kirsty made her

choice firmly, bound by female matters, today she found it easy to respond to the Queen's exuberance and warmth. Her voice was beautiful, deep for a woman, commanding and at the same time caressing with its faintly accented English. Beautiful too her hands, with long, white tapered fingers and nails of delicate pink. Beautiful fingers that were never idle, for she used her hands constantly in conversation, to illustrate a point, in the French manner.

This day she wore no wig as for ceremonial occasions and her lovely wavy hair was tied back with a ribbon. She wore a simple claret-coloured kirtle and matching petticoat, and occasionally yawned over her threads, for matters of state with the English ambassador, all the now tedious small details of arrangements of protocol and the like, for meeting Elizabeth of England, had kept her from her bed until late. Smiling, she apologised for kitten-soft yawns, stretching long slender arms above her head, drooping like a tired flower from its long slender neck.

As they sorted through swatches of materials, choosing colours from the rainbow of satins and velvets, spilling over arms and hands, gleaming, glistening like a living tide of radiance, Kirsty was aware again of a curious sense of time shrinking. When her royal mistress smiled, Kirsty was sure that this precise moment had happened before, and that this was not the first time they had sat together with Mary frowning over a choice of threads in the supper-room at Holyroodhouse.

"What think you now? The cramoisie?" asked Mary sweeping the satin across one shoulder. On the opposite wall a handsome Venetian mirror reflected her action and their two faces side by side.

It was the Queen's turn to shiver. She touched Kirsty's hand as if for reassurance. "You feel it too, *chérie?*"

"That this has happened before, Your Majesty?" whispered Kirsty.

The Queen nodded. "Aye, *déjà vu*, we call it in the French."

The candles had been lit against a day of cold and rain and

now the light turned their reflections into a haloed twin-image. Pale faces with the cramoisie satin like a blood-gash. There was something about this room, thought Kirsty, as if it waited for violence, held itself uneasily in readiness for some monstrous deed. She shivered, for the rain's whisper sounded like a death-rattle and the wind's angry clatter at the windows like the clash of swords.

She thought of all those Stuart kings who had died by violence, whose blood Mary had inherited, from Malcolm the Fair to her father King Jamie, who defeated at Solway Moss, had died of a broken heart and left his kingdom to a lass. An ill-fated family.

Mary smiled at Kirsty's image. "Do you miss Cramond?"

"I miss my grandfather, Your Majesty, not the place itself."

"My father had a fondness for it, and if your grandfather had not saved his life, there would be no more Stuart monarchs." She watched Kirsty for a moment. "Your mother, was she young and comely as yourself?"

"I know not, madam, for she died at my birth."

"Poor lass, God rest her soul."

The idea that King Jamie had fathered her was no longer as monstrous an idea when Kirsty gazed on the face of his legitimate daughter beside her. The truth was in her own blood, the thrill of passion that surged through her that she *was* Scotland, indivisible from mountain and stream, from heather slope to this great city of Edinburgh, this great stone palace.

A page entered, announcing that Lord James had returned from Stirling and wished an immediate audience with Her Majesty.

"Inform Lord James that I will see him directly."

Kirsty was curious about Lord James and how he would react to her presence of the serving-wench from the Ainslie Tavern, where they had briefly met.

"Now we shall have some sport," said the Queen and seizing Kirsty's arm, she thrust her into the royal chair. Covering her gown with one of the satin swathes, she removed her own coif and put it on Kirsty's head, tucking her blonde hair out of sight. Then clasping her hands with delight, she laughed at Kirsty's obvious bewilderment.

"And now let us see if my Lord James can recognise his own sister." Her smile was mischievous and laying a finger to her lips, she stood behind the door, stifling her laughter while Kirsty waited, heart thumping, eyes demurely lowered. The advancing steps across the audience chamber told her that Lord James now hovered above her, bowing.

"I returned as rapidly as I was able, madam. We will discuss Stirling in more detail when you are ready to make decisions on several important matters there. I gather that when I rode in last night, you were too tired to receive me to discuss the arrangements made thus far for your meeting with Elizabeth of England."

His tone was reproachful. It suggested that weariness was a moral defect in the Queen of Scots, a tiresome female weakness. He held up some documents. "I would beg you to consider these matters as urgent. Your cousin of England has long expressed great tenderness and regard for yourself and is more than willing to journey north for this meeting. But you must be prepared to meet her half-way. Her suggestions of a meeting-place are reasonable. Her statements that she wishes the meeting to be on the English side of the borders are also reasonable. 'Tis further from London to Carlisle, than from Edinburgh to Hermitage. What say you, madam? You asked for time to think."

Kirsty raised her eyes, opened her mouth, but no words would come. If she had to speak the Scots tongue of Cramond, then all deception ended.

"I have had all the time I need, my dear James," said Mary's voice from the doorway. Lord James spun round to stare at his half-sister and then back again in disbelief to the girl occupying her chair.

"Is this not a delightful charade?" asked the Queen, taking Lord James' arm and kissing his cheek. "You were deceived, were you not?" Solemnly now she regarded Kirsty. "And if you were deceived, why not others who know me less well? This game we play has limitless possibilities, agree you not, Howison? What think you?"

"If it pleases Your Majesty," whispered Kirsty.

"And what think you of this meeting with Her Majesty, my cousin of England?" asked the Queen smiling. "Shall we decide upon Hermitage?"

"Madam," said James warningly.

The Queen held up a hand. "She shall decide, my lord."

Kirsty shook her head. "I cannot, Your Majesty. I beg you excuse such a decision, for I know naught of politics, or of what is involved in such a meeting."

The Queen clapped her hands together. "Well said and wisely spoken; would that others in my court were as firmly disposed to give advice reluctantly when they knew not the matter in hand. Now, James, 'tis your turn to speak. But first, what think you of my little trick? Stand up, *chérie*, let Lord James see you in a proper light."

Lord James regarded Kirsty sourly. "An excellent imposture, but for the voice and stature." And as the Queen removed the coif from Kirsty's head, "The hair colour too." Eyes brooding, he said thoughtfully: "But seated and silent, she is your double." Turning to his royal half-sister, he asked: "What play-acting have you in mind, madam, that you present me with such a trick?"

The Queen shrugged. "Naught but innocent pleasure, my lord. At the moment. There are dreary occasions when I must appear at pageants and masques, where I would rather be elsewhere, when I am weary or indisposed but must sit politely smiling through interminable speeches. It occurs to me, having seen how readily you accepted Kirsty as myself, that others would do so too. This likeness would be convenient and the deception would hurt no one. If Howison is agreeable," she added hastily, and the sunny smile she darted in Kirsty's direction made disagreement impossible.

"I like it not, madam," he said harshly. Then studying Kirsty's features carefully, he added. "Might one ask whence comes this curious likeness?"

"You must treat Howison kindly, my lord, for she is of our blood; another sibling of ours, another issue of our royal father's well-flung seed."

Lord James frowned and bowed coldly in Kirsty's direction, hating as always the reminder of his royal bastardy. In his face Kirsty saw little resemblance to the Queen except in the eyes. Again her instinct told her that he was a cold, austere man, and an ambitious one. A man to be feared, despite his apparent devotion to the Queen.

" 'Tis not the first time you have met Kirsty Howison. Remember, the Ainslie Tavern, when we were taken in the storm?"

"I need no reminders, madam. 'Tis ill-fitting that a Queen should strut about the town in lad's apparel like a play-actor." As the Queen opened her mouth to protest at this criticism, Lord James swung round to face Kirsty. "So you are Jock Howison's granddaughter, domiciled at Cramond."

"He is dead, James," said the Queen softly.

"What do you here?"

"I am handfasted to Dirk Farr, Lord Laverock, sir."

Lord James gave a bark of mirthless laughter. "The gipsy laird?"

"He is none the worse for that," said the Queen sharply, "My brave *Garde Ecossaise*. And his parents were legally married, so I am told."

Kirsty saw Lord James wince at this second reminder of his bastardy. However, he recovered quickly and spread his hands wide in a helpless gesture. "Then you must do as you wish, madam, regarding your new acquisition, for I cannot advise you on this any more than upon the weightier matters which should be occupying your attention at the present time."

The Queen ignored the reproach. "Very well. Then we shall try out our player upon a larger audience. And we shall not have long to wait. At noon, a deputation of new burgesses comes to present me with a declaration of their loyalty. Howison shall receive them for me."

"I beg of you, madam, this is folly."

"Nonsense, James, we have to begin somewhere, after all."

And so at noon, from the balcony of the state apartments, Kirsty Howison prepared to smile graciously upon the burgesses. She was more apprehensive about the townsfolk who had flocked after them; Queen Mary was the crowd's darling and the lasses cheered her as loudly as did their men.

"The Queen! The Queen!

"God bless our bonny lass!"

The crowd detected another movement behind the revealing glass panes. The window opened. A gasp of delight was followed by a cheer from every throat as the Queen of Scots, their bonny Mary, leaned out, and smiling, held out her hands in greeting. They recognised the bright auburn curls, the white coif and black velvet mourning gown. They felt compassion for this child-wife who had become a girl-widow when her husband King Francis had died a few days before her eighteenth birthday. Both still children they had been too. And within the year her mother, Good Marie de Guise, had died and the Dowager Queen of France was Queen of Scotland and the Isles.

"God bless Your Majesty – long reign to you – long life – aye, long life."

"O ye daughter of Babylon, corrupt and full of sins!"

The voice was high, querulous, but Kirsty shivered as it thundered through the crowd who obediently fell silent and made way for the black-clad figure with white Geneva bands, the straggling white beard and black bonnet.

They knew him well and feared him too. Women curtseyed to the Minister of St Giles, while their men avoided the rheumy but fierce eyes of Master John Knox, whose long sharp nose seemed capable of sniffing out adulterers. They watched fascinated as Master Knox strode forward, and hands on hips, stood glaring up at the regal figure in the window.

"Vanity, saith the Lord, all is vanity. He shall smite thee hip and thigh. Woe to all the ungodly, the sinful, the lustful.

None shall escape His vengeance. Not kings, nor queens, madam. Remember the fate of Queen Jezebel."

The Queen's smiling face was seen to tremble, as did the hand she held out as though to ward off a blow.

"Shame on you, Master Knox – shame!"

At the sound of that deep voice, the crowd swivelled round and made way for the tall man who pushed forward to the minister's side. He wore the uniform of the *Garde Ecossaise*.

Even in the crowd of Edinburgh townsfolk, Kirsty, looking down on Dirk Farr, decided that he made an impressive sight. Tall, black-haired, his eyes crystal-bright, cold above a curved nose and generous mouth. Thick black brows like devil's wings, a barbaric single golden earring—

The crowd made way for him and Kirsty fancied that those nearest shivered as his shadow touched them. Many had heard whispers that the new Lord Laverock was a warlock. Now black-clad, did that long swirling velvet cape cover a cloven hoof?

"Aye, he's black enough to have the devil's own mark on him."

"An Egyptian." The voice was contemptuous.

"I hear tell his Da was a respectable Christian, who married a gipsy lass."

" 'Twas all done by witchcraft, I'll surmise – Shh—"

The soldier and the minister, extremes in everything, faced each other like bristling angry dogs. The Queen was seen to be nervous and the crowd prepared to enjoy themselves, hoping for a fight. Doubtless Master Knox's presence had upset the poor lass with his canting and shouting, for she smiled once more and with an inclination of her head, vanished back into the state gallery.

"Shame upon you, Master Knox, for haranguing your rightful Queen as if she were some fishwife." Dirk Farr did not trouble to lower his voice, which resounded heavily upon the minister's ears.

"I owe allegiance to none but God himself, only God rules John Knox. Aye, God and his Holy Word, which bids us hold fast against idolators – and fornicators." He made a sweeping gesture towards the crowd. "Get ye to your homes. Be done with sinful idleness – pray for forgiveness—"

The crowd obeyed reluctantly, those furthest from the minister murmuring to each other and all hoping that the Queen might reappear and take Master Knox to task. They had heard their bonny lass could hold her own on the matter of argument about religious doctrines and the Bible too.

"Go – I command you."

This time they obeyed him, and those glancing back at the royal windows would have been surprised indeed had they been witnesses to the scene taking place therein.

As "the Queen of Scots" closed the casement with trembling hands, the real Queen came forward.

"You have done well, Howison. We are pleased with you. They really believe 'twas myself they saw and they cheered, to the last man." Laughing, she took Kirsty's hands. "There is no need for fear, *ma petite*, the worst is over."

"The worst, madam?"

The Queen smiled reassuringly. "The first time – that is worst. But you have played your part superbly, and shall do again, many times. At least we know that our charade can – and will – succeed."

"But, madam, Master Knox – I had no thought he would be there."

"Fie upon Master Knox," said the Queen, snapping her fingers. "He could not tell the difference, nor could Dirk Farr. Stay," she added as Kirsty was about to remove the auburn wig. "Let us see how our bodyguard greets his Queen."

"He will know, madam, for sure," Kirsty demurred.

"Come, you would not deprive me of a little amusement, Howison." Mary's smile was beguilingly impish. "After all, 'tis but a game, an innocent deception."

The door opened to admit Dirk Farr, and the Queen withdrew to the shadows. He bowed low towards the regal figure seated at the window.

"Your Majesty."

Bewildered, Kirsty faced him across the floor.

"Find Seton and send her to me at once." The voice was the Queen's.

"Immediately, madam."

As the door closed upon Dirk Farr, the Queen darted forward and seized Kirsty's hands. "What say you to that, Howison? First, my brother, then Master Knox and now my own bodyguard." She smiled slyly. "If you can deceive him, then our little charade is certain of success." She gave Kirsty an appraising glance. "But for the colour of our hair and our differing heights, we could be not only sisters, but twins."

Only months separated them in age and this fact intrigued the Queen. "But then, the late king my father had an eye always for a pretty face." Glancing towards the door which opened to admit Lord James, she whispered, laughing: "He was not always fortunate in the result."

She ran to her half-brother's side, kissing his cheek and tucking an affectionate hand into his arm. "See, James, we succeeded, as I told you we would. And beyond all hopes. For Howison deceived not only the burgesses, but Master Knox – and her betrothed. She was magnificent – I wish you had been present."

"I was, madam. I had the pleasure of watching your little charade with Master Knox." His bow to Kirsty was chilly. "However, he delayed me with tiresome fulminations against the Mass being said, or I would have been here directly." Critically he eyed Kirsty. "You can indeed fool the people that you are Her Majesty – from a distance. As long as you keep your mouth closed and remain seated."

Kirsty shivered. She was no play-actor, nor a mimic like the Queen's female jesters. She could never hope to imitate the Queen's beautiful cultured voice, not in a hundred years. Even high-born nobles would have found great difficulty in disguising their strong Scots accents.

"This imposture, madam," Lord James continued, "what hope you to gain further from it?"

The Queen pouted prettily. "Nought, brother, 'tis but a

whim, a caprice which will save me wearying through yet another of Master Knox's dreary morality plays, indicating the hellfire in store for those who would hear the Mass. To think that such worthy sentiments will fall upon Kirsty's ears who needs no conversion, will bring me immeasurable pleasure." She sighed. "And think too of those endless pageants and masques I have to suffer from a draughty dais on the High Street. Howison's imposture will buy me leisure and freedom."

There was a little silence before Lord James spoke again. "Make sure, madam," he said slowly, "that none but the essential actors in your charade know of this deception – innocent as it is, such knowledge would go ill with your people's love and trust, should you appear in two places at the same time."

The Queen laughed. "Then we would have to blame Dirk Farr – and his splendid reputation as a warlock," she said with a mischievous glance in Kirsty's direction.

They should not laugh about such things, thought Kirsty in horror. She was suddenly afraid, watching the solemn face of Lord James, that what had begun as an innocent royal prank might have dire consequences not only upon the Queen of Scots, but upon herself.

As if aware of Kirsty's distress, the Queen was suddenly serious too.

"You are quite right, James. I wish to offend none, and it shall be as you wish. None shall know beyond this room that it was Kirsty Howison who received the town's burgesses today. It shall be our little secret. Do you agree, Howison?"

"I do, Your Majesty."

"You understand that not even Dirk Farr is to be told."

"I do, Your Majesty."

"Can you keep such a secret from him, do you think?"

"If it is Your Majesty's wish."

Mary beamed. It would please her to tease Dirk Farr a little. She enjoyed the prospect of having a secret shared with Kirsty in which he was not included, as she also shared his secret which excluded Kirsty. Such small intrigues, so harmless, passed the days most agreeably and broke the monotony of state matters.

As for Kirsty, she looked from one to the other, the laughing Queen, the secret face of the Earl of Moray. An uneasy dread filled her that it would not always be like this, light-hearted and amusing. Some day, someone would try to gain by her imposture, for she knew that the Queen's wish to keep the matter secret was folly, that sooner rather than later, all secrets became public property within the walls of the palace.

Most afternoons when the weather was tolerable, she escaped from her silken prison to walk in the Queen's private gardens where the Maries exercised the royal dogs. Kirsty enjoyed this hour of relaxation, even when she was masked against the sunshine, a habit she deplored. However, the Queen's ladies insisted and she suspected, in her own case, that the request included the fear that two many eyes might notice her resemblance to the Queen.

She found herself looking forward to the occasions on which Dirk joined them in the garden, although she was careful to remain distant towards him. Curtseying in the formal manner which so many prying eyes demanded, seeing how they both behaved as strangers to one another, the other Kirsty, who had inherited the passionate wild Stuart blood from her royal father, ached to behave in less restrained manner, craving warm looks and warmer lips from my lord Laverock.

Each time they met she was hopeful that some word, some tenderness would dispel the barrier which continued to grow higher at every meeting. She prayed for the miracle to turn them into the lovers whose stories, oft-times sad and tragic-ended, the Queen's musicians sang in the court ballads. Star-crossed these lovers might be, but she sighed with envy for the brief candle of such a love to span all eternity.

But her sighs and prayers were in vain, the proud, arrogant Dirk Farr remained aloof. Alas, she had no means of reading his mind and might have been consoled to learn that he suffered in like manner, ashamed of his uncouth gipsy manners, for which he believed she despised him. Events of late between them had been so painful that he was afraid to open his mouth in case some ill-chosen word condemned him for ever in her eyes, or threw her into a cold-faced rage.

Knowing not what to do, he took refuge in the safe topic, harmonious to both of them, the welfare of the Queen of Scots.

"Her Majesty needs time for leisure, which she rarely gets," Kirsty observed. "She is often indisposed, sick at heart as well as in body!"

She had been alarmed at first to see that the Queen suffered from strange maladies, exhaustion, high and inexplicable fevers that laid her low for days at a time. From the Maries she learned not to be unduly anxious, for the Queen had suffered such "humours" from childhood, baffling physicians in France and now in Scotland also. Long ago, when nothing would stay upon Mary's stomach, the royal chef had invented a new concoction. She had always craved oranges, and so he heated the fruit in a pan, stirred in honey for sweetening and to give her strength. When he was asked the name of this conserve he shrugged and said: "I call it Marie Malade." The court had shortened this to "Mar'malade" and it had now taken its place of honour in the royal kitchen.

No matter how ill Mary Stuart felt, she was always able to put on a "fine face" for ceremonial purposes. She could not bear to disappoint her people or fail to appear at an audience. Her changes of mood baffled Kirsty.

"First she is high in the air, laughing and radiant, happy and hopeful, then without warning, she takes to her bed, sighing, pale and tearful."

"She was ever thus. 'Tis well known," said Dirk Farr unfeelingly. "But this meeting with the English Queen, I like it not." He shook his head frowning. "The old Tudor vixen is devious. There could be danger in it."

"Danger?" The word echoed, shaking the blossom petals

across their path as they strolled through the orchard. Dirk
Farr broke off a slender twig, twirling it between his fingers
and scattering the delicate petals. "Danger," whispered
Kirsty, "how so?"

The word had frightened her, as did his destruction of the
flower. She longed to seize his hands, lock his arms about
her. She longed to listen to words of reassurance that no harm
would come to any of them, that no corruption or evil lay
behind the placid sunlit walls of the palace. She wished him
to tell her that the world of Queen Mary and Holyroodhouse
would remain for ever as pretty and innocent as this perfect
summer's day.

"Surely you can see what this meeting entails. Her Majesty
is honest and forthright and believes 'her dear sister of
England' to be so. Her Majesty trusts those around her
in whom she confides, but there might well be those in the
court who seek to use this meeting to their own advantage, as a stepping-stone to their ambitions," he added
uneasily.

"You mean – Lord James?" When he said nothing she
added: "Surely you are mistaken. He is her half-brother."

He laughed mirthlessly. "A fact which never kept any
royal household from murder, if you know your history
books. He covets her throne, the man's ambition is bound-
less," he added bluntly.

Kirsty was shocked. "He loves her."

"True, he appears to do so. But never forget that he
bitterly resents her sovereignty. He can never forgive or
forget the irony of fate, the bastardy which for ever separates
him from the Crown of Scotland. 'Tis worse, since he
knows that his father truly loved Margaret Douglas and
would willingly have married her, but he was forced to
abandon her for a political marriage to Marie de Guise,
Mary's mother. Men like James of Moray do not forget or
forgive readily."

He pointed to the Maries, whose distant laughter rang
across the grass where they romped with the Queen's lap-
dogs.

"As for those sweet creatures, 'tis true they would die for her, but they are so guileless that any clever, devious man, could obtain the information he needed with little difficulty – especially a man whose loyalty was to the English Queen," he added significantly.

When she did not reply, he continued: "As for Master Armstrong, I wonder if he is altogether trustworthy, for all his blithe and honest countenance. I doubt whether he tells his own heart of his desires in case that same heart betrays him."

"You are wrong," Kirsty protested. "He is a good kind man."

He smiled bleakly. "So one would think, as Master Armstrong wishes us to do."

It was contemptible, she thought angrily, that he should follow the like manner of so many of the Queen's courtiers, that devotion to Her Majesty should lead to jealousy over Master Armstrong or any other man who was in her confidence. She had thought Dirk Farr beyond such small meannesses.

"Remember that diplomacy is a cloak Master Armstrong has worn so many years that it now fits him like an extra skin," he added grimly.

Master Armstrong was the one man in court she would trust, Kirsty thought. She would put her life into his hands without questions, for he alone had showed that he understood her loneliness, her desperate need for the comfort of friends amongst all these posturing strangers. Useless to try to convey this to Dirk Farr. She said instead: "That sounds like wilful spite, my lord, and unworthy of you."

With a calm she was far from feeling, she turned on her heel to leave him. He seized her arm and stared down into her face, like a man who searches for something he has lost. She saw only cold anger in his eyes and despaired. Was there to be nought but bitterness between them, was every meeting to be soured by angry words? Could they never find the laughter that came so readily to other lovers?

"When you choose to weave dangerous friendships, then

remember that I am responsible for you, that my reputation is linked with your own."

"Remember!" she cried, "I wish in God's name, that someone – some day – would allow me to forget!"

She heard the despair in her voice following her like an echo as she ran to where the Maries beckoned. She did not get very far. Dirk Farr caught up with her and putting an arm around her, drew her head against his breast, cradling her like a small unhappy child. For a moment his action stirred that other echo of memory, the night her grandfather had died and she had clung to him, sobbing, alone and needing comfort.

She reached out her arms to him in welcome. Hands on his shoulders, she raised her mouth for the kiss that would close out all her fears, end for ever her isolation. His lips brushed hers and with a small sigh, she began to drown in the passion of longing his nearness brought.

"Howison – Howison!" The voices belonged to the Maries.

Kirsty opened her eyes, found Dirk Farr staring ahead. "Forgive me, we should not quarrel. I have only your interests at heart. Your welfare—"

Kirsty could have wept. Interests and welfare, when she wanted the ecstasy of love that his kisses promised! She drew herself up with pride, for she was her royal father's daughter, and she stared at him with defiance and contempt.

"*My* interests, my lord? Are you not confusing such emotions with the greed of a common gipsy to possess the Queen's half-sister? A prize worth the boasting in any tavern."

His grip on her arm made her cry out. "That is not true," he whispered, teeth clenched upon his rage.

"You know it is true, my lord, unless you are a liar too. For I have it from your own lips."

His hands slid down her arms and she felt their warmth burning into her, reaching her own betraying heart which cried out for him.

"I have some affection for you—"

"Howison – Howison! Come, the Queen awaits."

Kirsty stared helplessly at the distant figures of the Maries, waving anxiously as they hurried towards the palace. She raised a hand, indicating that she had heard, that she was coming. In that moment she hated them, hated the posturing forms of duty. Duty, when she longed to be free to be simply Kirsty Howison of Cramond again.

And here before her was this man, the author of present woes, her future husband, her inescapable owner, offering her "some affection". It was beyond bearing!

"Have you then no such regard for me?"

Looking away towards the Maries, biting her lips angrily, she did not observe the torture in his eyes. Her shrug was cold, heartless indifference.

"Regard, my lord? Nay, I have only contempt for you. Since I have you to thank for being held here against my will, away from my friends and all those I love, I hate and despise you."

His hands dropped to his sides as if she had struck him a mortal blow. He did not try to stop her flight, and when she reached the Maries, she saw that he had not moved but stood like a man turned to stone.

Watching him across the distance, she wished the words unsaid, wished with all her heart that he did not arouse such feelings of passionate rage in her. For he was unlike any man she had ever met before, and had the woeful circumstances of their forced handfasting been otherwise, she might have looked upon him favourably – given time.

Mary Stuart was particular that her Protestant servants in the palace walked up the Royal Mile to attend divine service at St. Giles' Church each Sunday, so that Master Knox might not accuse her of seducing them from the Reformed Faith. Now, as Kirsty listened to the names of Moses, David and Solomon with all his wives, of great Biblical prophets and lost angels, it was not Master Knox's face she beheld in the pulpit, but that of Dirk Farr.

The face of a man from an alien race, as though long-forgotten folk-heroes had sired him and lost from the earth, he had been overlooked in their departure and left to wander the lanes of the world alone.

And the thought gave her, as well as fear, compassion for his loneliness.

CHAPTER
EIGHT

QUEEN MARY had received the news she eagerly awaited. Her patience had been rewarded, and Elizabeth of England had graciously agreed to cross the Scottish borders to greet "her dear sister of Scotland".

Each summer, the English Queen progressed north from Greenwich Palace, economising on the royal purse by enjoying the hospitality of her nobles in their fine castles and mansions. She was to sojourn in Cumberland at Carlisle Castle and would set out thence and travel incognito to a secret place one day's ride north. This place agreed upon by the two Queens would be under secret seal until the time appointed. As proof of her "love and honourable intent" Elizabeth would take with her a small escort only, essential to her comfort and well-being upon the journey. She expected her "dear sister" to do likewise.

Both Queens were in agreement that since it was summertime, a meeting out of doors would provide privacy and informality, which they desired. There were many final and close-guarded arrangements to be made, since anti-Royalist factions existed in both countries and should either sovereign be abducted or assassinated, then bloody war would follow between their two countries. And neither Mary nor Elizabeth had any wish for war. On that they were in complete agreement, and this need for peaceful co-existence was the motivation for their secret meeting.

To Kirsty, with her neat and exquisite stitches, came the task of making a collection of fine garments to be worn next the English Queen's delicate skin. Mary had brought with her exquisite linen from France and Kirsty was instructed to make as well as petticoats and shifts, drawers embroidered with the English rose and the Scottish thistle.

Few Scots, even in noble houses, were aware of such finery already prevalent in the French court, since drawers had been the scandalous introduction of Catherine de' Medici, who wore them under her petticoats. Such a garment in satin and finest lace would Mary present to her sister of England.

She smiled, knowing that such would please the saucy English Queen who would not hesitate, from all accounts, to show it to her courtiers, since her coarseness of tongue and her shocking behaviour caused Court ladies to wilt.

There was one unbroken rule which everyone at the palace had to observe. Once they had supped the day's anxieties and cares were put aside, and the Queen's "Little France" came into its own. For a few hours each evening, the court enjoyed a way of life which would have surprised most noble households by its culture and gaiety.

Night was turned back into day by the extravagant light of scores of white scented candles, each a foot high and thick as a man's fist. There were French songs and poems, and a lute's sweet notes as accompaniment. The four Maries, whose voices were charming, sang *Chansons Champêtres* or round songs. Then came madrigals from the courtiers while the Queen's female jesters tumbled and postured, obviously aping the more illustrious members of the absent and solemn Scots aristocracy, judging by the gales of merriment and applause that their antics provoked. Chosen for their wit as well as their agility, they gabbled in a shrill and fast French dialect which even those who knew French well could not understand.

However, their gestures sometimes made very explicit the matter under discussion, much to Kirsty's embarrassment.

The round games, also in French, were beyond Kirsty, since they required quick wit and considerable knowledge of subtle rhyming. She fared better at cards, but preferred to be an onlooker, to watch others and in particular to listen to the Queen reading the poems of Ronsard.

Although Kirsty could not understand the words, the Queen's voice was unforgettable, touching and beautiful. Often as the applause died away, she saw her dash away a tear from her cheek and sigh. For Mary Stuart was homesick for the land across the sea, and would always be so. Nostalgic for a life when she had been Dauphiness, then Queen – for a brief time – and finally Dowager, and all before the age of eighteen. Then her own mother Marie de Guise, the Regent of Scotland, had died, and the girl-widow-Queen of France had become Queen of Scotland and the Isles.

But such melancholy was rare, mostly the air was filled with merriment and youthful hope and joy, the promise that old age would never overtake any of them and with their Queen they would continue to live in an enchanted world, changeless and immortal.

One evening with guard-duty at an end, the Queen invited Dirk Farr to join them. Since their disastrous encounter in the Queen's garden, Kirsty had been careful to avoid Dirk, and suspected that he was no more eager for her society than she was for his. The Queen, however, with the soft heart for lovers, as she believed them to be, seized Kirsty's hand and gave her a gentle push in Dirk's direction.

"Go, *ma chérie*, and sit by your lord."

A place was made for her at his side and this close bodily contact in the crowded room stung Kirsty into embarrassed silence. Dirk fared no better, his face remaining impassive. For the sake of the watchers who smiled benevolently upon them, he gently drew her arm within his own, hoping that a certain reserve or lack of enthusiasm was doubtless dismissed as Scots reserve where the emotions of the heart were concerned.

They soon became the target of the female jester's wit, whose warm glances and coy endearments clearly alarmed Dirk Farr, who spoke French fluently. When he did not respond Kirsty saw their impish merriment increase, and he was very put out by the graphic nature of their speech and their rather broad gestures, which even she, blushing, could not fail to understand.

One evening Fleming told her to prepare for a special celebration.

"A birthday celebration, Howison," she said pointedly when Kirsty's face looked blank.

"Oh – whose birthday, Mistress Fleming?"

The Queen's housekeeper regarded her, hands on hips. "Whose? You might well ask, Howison. 'Tis my lord Laverock's, who else? Now hurry!" But as she left she gave Kirsty a very odd look, clearly wondering what betrothed folk talked about when they were ignorant of each other's birthdays.

Kirsty realised that she had nothing to give him, but her embarrassment went unobserved, since all believed that as a handfasted couple, they did enjoy some private life. She often wondered where any in the palace found time to be private, except during the night. And she blushed at the thought that the Queen and her servants had obviously given her a bedchamber of her own for that very purpose.

As it was Dirk Farr's birthday, he was called upon to sing at the Queen's command. She was surprised into admiration for his deep lilting voice as he sang the strange wild songs of the gipsies, and her applause was unfeigned.

"Will you tell our fortunes, my lord, since this is a special occasion?" asked Livingstone, ignoring the knowing glances that were exchanged, and the giggles too. Whispers were going about the court that the Queen's Secretary of State, Maitland of Lethington, was casting amorous glances on the voluptuous Livingstone.

Dirk Farr smiled and stretched out his hand. "Most willingly." He turned her palm over and was silent. She watched his face anxiously, and then he smiled and began to tell her of a marriage.

The other Maries clustered around him and the female jesters, one of whom whispered to Kirsty: "Zis man of yours, you are lucky – he could make his fortune as a sorcerer. We were in France with ze Queen and he foretold ze deaths of the Dauphin and ze Queen's mother, almost to ze day."

From the laughter and delighted cries issuing from the

group clustered around him, his present prophecies contained no such dire events.

At last the Maries emerged and Livingstone went to the Queen and said:

"Madam, let him tell your future."

The Queen looked up at him and Kirsty saw an expression that was almost a plea for mercy. In a moment it was gone.

"I think not, Livingstone. Another time perhaps, my lord Laverock."

"Then Howison here – she shall know her future."

"Nay, Mistress Livingstone," laughed Dirk Farr.

"Let us hope she knows that already," said the Queen smiling, and Kirsty felt a strange surge of relief.

The night was warm and the singing over they began to dance. There was little room for such activity, and someone called:

Au jardin—au jardin—— The cry was taken up, and out to the garden they tripped, down the twisting staircase, each clinging, giggling to the waist of the one in front, a great winding human chain. In the twilight where the first stars rose into an azure sky, the maids in pale billowing skirts, white-ruffed, moved like huge moths and the breeze touching the courtiers' bright velvet cloaks with their satin lacings turned them into strange exotic creatures, winged insects of the approaching dark.

Blind Man's Buff was the game chosen by popular request.

Kirsty was seized, and with a scarf about her eyes spun, again and again. Dizzily she snatched at air and then encountered a velvet sleeve. The players cheered: "Bravo – bravo! Who goes there?" They chanted, "A kiss, a kiss for the blind man. Guess, guess who kisses thee, and only then shall ye be free."

She felt warm breath on her cheek and was about to reach out her hands and trace the face before her. However, she found her arms were held fast to her sides. The lips that descended and found her own were warm and tender. The kiss was gentle at first and them more exploratory. Suddenly she did not want to escape, she did not want to guess, longing only for the warmth, the voluptuous comfort of those lips again.

To have such kisses from a lover, what kind of man must he be, so worldly-wise and yet so tender? She stifled a moan of pleasure as the warm mouth descended again and his hands gently slid down her bare arms. As he let her go at last, she found that she was trembling.

"Who kisses thee, guess and be free," chanted the players. Kirsty shook her head.

"A forfeit – a forfeit, then!"

"What will you give me, Kirsty Howison?" The voice was but a whisper and as the scarf was taken from her eyes she looked, lips still burning, into the bright steel-cold eyes of Dirk Farr. She gasped and raised a hand to her mouth. That so much coldness could exist upon the same face as these ravishing kisses! She thought of the other times he had kissed her, with compassion when her grandfather died, with savage anger the night before she came to Holyroodhouse. She had never dreamed that he could be tender – so tender – too.

She was aware of the ring of silent players as they stared into each other's eyes. The onlookers watched them strangely, nudging and exchanging glances as Dirk Farr turned on his heel and walked away. She was certain there would be many whispers later, and even more speculation as to why Kirsty Howison had not known and recognised the lips of her betrothed.

"Again, again," said the players circling around her. "She did not guess. The blind man is not free yet."

Humiliated, her face burning with shame, she allowed the scarf to be tied once more. It was some time before she seized a sleeve and a strong arm.

"Guess, guess – who is he?"

This time no one pinned back her arms, she raised her hands and touched rough hair, a lined brow, a moustache. Together with a certain shortness of breath these denoted Master Nigel Armstrong.

When she said his name, a gasp and a sigh escaped the

watchers. The scarf was unwound and she saw that the looks of amusement on the players' faces. How had Kirsty Howison known Master Armstrong, who was old enough to be her father, and not recognised the kisses of the man to whom she was handfasted?

"For shame," someone whispered.

Only one man did not smile. From the edge of the ring, Kirsty saw Dirk Farr's chilly countenance and his eyes asking the same question. How had she known Master Armstrong?

"A forfeit for the blind man," chanted the players.

Master Armstrong laughed. Smiling, he leaned forward and kissing her forehead, patted her cheek and walked away to where the Queen beckoned.

Kirsty watched the Queen put a hand on his arm and smile into his face. Gone tonight was the cloak of majesty; she was a young girl happy and at ease among young friends of like minds.

When they returned to the royal apartments they found her dictating a letter which Master Armstrong was to carry to Elizabeth. As she sought the right words, her voice carried excitement and longing. "If God will grant a good occasion – that we might meet together – which we wish may be soon – we trust you shall more clearly perceive the – sincerity of our good meaning – than we can express by letter."

During the days that followed messengers rode in reporting on the English Queen's progress while Mary behaved like a small child excited by a promised treat. A dozen times a day she consulted her mirror, exclaimed anxiously over her hair, over an unexpected blemish on that flawless skin. She examined her features in great detail, frowning and sighing, hoping that she would be well and in good spirits and would look her very best, so that her "dear sister" would love her the more.

The four Maries exchanged wry glances at her innocence.

"Does she not realise that those tales of her legendary beauty are what makes Elizabeth of England resent her most?"

"Aye, she has all that the English Queen lacks and most desires."

"Beauty, youth – and our sweet Queen has known love, has been a wife," sighed Livingstone.

Overhearing this conversation, Kirsty had the idea that the middle-aged virgin Queen would have been better pleased to meet an ill-visaged dwarf than the lovely Queen of Scots.

A week before the meeting, an unexpected hazard was thrown into the preparations when news reached Holyrood that "the new Influence" was rife in Edinburgh, and that many households had fallen victim to this strange sweating fever. Panic had seized the townsfolk. They barred their doors and would not venture over the thresholds, all windows were shuttered against the putrid air and market days were abandoned. They knew cholera and typhus and feared that this unknown was the outbreak of another pestilence, one of the misfortunes of strong summer sunshine and rainless days upon the middens, with their abundant flies and putrid odours.

It was observed, however, that after a few days most folk recovered and were none the worse for the attack, although a little weak in the legs and lacking in appetite. The only deaths reported were among the old or invalid. It was further noticed that the "new Influence" did not strike young children, and those who nursed the afflicted often escaped themselves.

The Queen, after a consultation with her physicians, refused, as Lord James begged, that she should close the gates of Holyroodhouse firmly against the town at least until her Border meeting. The Maries added their pleas and moaned: "What will happen if your Majesty takes ill and cannot leave next week?"

Obstinately the Queen shook her head, her eyes glowing with health and excitement. "*Mes petites*, we are in the good Lord's hands. He will take care of us."

There was another reason, the Maries suspected, for the Queen's radiance. A radiance which extended down the corridors in a flutter of excitement among the humblest maids.

James Hepburn, the Earl of Bothwell and the Queen's most loyal servant, had arrived at court to arrange the final details of the Border meeting, for the Queen and her retinue were to lodge at Hermitage Castle.

Kirsty, hearing these whispers, decided that the Earl must indeed be presentable from the many bright eyes and eager countenances around her. And ignoring the warnings of the "new Influence" rife in Edinburgh, the Queen decided to open the gates of the palace and hold a summer revel in my lord Bothwell's honour. The servants, the entire royal household, involved as they were in preparation for the Queen's departure to the Borders, threw up their hands in despair and fell to the task of preparing a royal banquet.

Evening came and the good weather held, mercifully answering the prayers of the main participants, for such a crowd of guests could not be accommodated within the palace. Kirsty found she was no longer needed as the four Maries took over the task of preparing the Queen in all her finery for the night's activities. And so from her room directly above the royal apartments, Kirsty watched the guests arrive, walking or riding over the drawbridge into the main courtyard.

Strains of music reached her ears and candles blazed forth a welcome, although it was not yet completely dusk. She sighed; so this was to be all she might enjoy of the Queen's Revel. How lovely to have been born a lady so that she might have had her part to play in the scene below! She thought wistfully of the accident of birth by which a king made one daughter a royal princess and the other a servant.

She heard footsteps on the stair above and giggling outside her door, and opening it she beheld the flushed countenances of the other seamstresses.

"Come with us, Kirsty. There is a wee corner by the minstrels' gallery where we go to watch the dancing."

She followed them willingly, and soon they all gazed down upon the long gallery where the tinkling of lutes, the sweet-voiced singers and the laughter of guests vividly dressed, mingled in a scene of animation and delight. Kirsty felt it touch her, even as an observer. She had never before been present at a gathering of the distinguished nobles of Scotland, nor would she again have such an opportunity. Every corner held some magnificent scene which she tried to remember later in exact detail. The bright gleam of hundreds of candles turned evening into day, each in many-branched silver sconces, on tables covered in fine linen cloths and napkins embroidered with the royal cipher.

The sight took her breath away, and she no longer minded in the least being a servant; she felt happy and privileged just to be present on such a grand occasion.

She saw that the long tables gleamed also with heavy gold and silver dishes, wreathed in daffodils and the bright flowers of early summer, which filled the air with gentle perfume, sparkling like lamps in the shadows while boughs heavy with blossom turned the gallery into a stage set for a play.

A sudden silence, an air of expectancy as all heads were turned towards the door leading to the royal apartments. As the Queen entered, Kirsty felt her heart beat faster and understood the familiarity of that first encounter between them, for in seeing Mary of Scotland's face it was as if she, Kirsty Howison, stared into a distant mirror at her own reflection.

Tonight the Queen had shed her mourning, for this was a private occasion with her friends. In public she would continue to wear black, grey or purple until she married again, reminding all that she was the Dowager Queen of France, widow of the young King Francis. And Kirsty knew that the Queen's joy in escaping from the sombre colours was as great as her own.

The gown she had chosen was exquisite, a robe of gold satin, puffed and ruched with a jewelled stomacher and an underskirt of emerald green. Upon her hair, a magnificent auburn wig, perched a small coronet in which the emeralds and diamonds caught the candlelight.

With the entire court bowing, curtseying before her, she walked the length of the gallery to where, on a raised dais, a throned chair bore upon its canopy the arms of Scotland and

France. Courtiers flocked to her side, hiding her from Kirsty's view.

She gave her attention to the other guests and saw the royal court of Scotland in all its splendour, the colours of the rainbow, despite the informality of the occasion, which the Queen had proclaimed, as a masked revel. Few of the nobles had travelled further than the handsome houses and towers bordering Edinburgh's High Street. Since Mary had come to her kingdom, the shrewd Scots lairds found it necessary, for their ambition's sake, to abandon far-flung estates in Fife, Angus or Aberdeen and build houses close to the royal court.

Sighing over the Queen's splendour, one of the maids whispered: "I wonder if Her Majesty will choose a husband soon?"

Her companion nodded. "Yon nobles have hopes, ye ken, either for themselves or for their sons, although she must have a royal prince."

"There she is now, leading the dance. See, Kirsty, the tallest woman in the gallery."

The Queen's partner matched her for height; his hair was dark auburn and despite the magnificence of velvet cape and satin doublet, he had a quality of steel, which Kirsty recognised.

It set her searching the shadows for the *Garde Ecossaise*. However, there was an anonymity about those sentinels tonight and she could not see which was Dirk Farr. She looked again at the Queen's partner, aware of the quality which denied the softness of courtier, the same undeniable and frightening power of masculinity which Dirk Farr exuded. Both men, she thought, could reduce the painted throng of Mary's French court to figures cut from paper.

"He is magnificent," she whispered. "Who is he?"

"What – him? Kirsty, he is a nobody. A mere Border laird."

"Aye, but he's bonny," said another maid sighing. "The Earl of Bothwell." And Kirsty understood the quiver of excitement his presence had brought as the maid continued:

"Did ye not hear, he's most likely to be Her Majesty's host at Hermitage Castle while she meets the English Queen?"

So much for secrecy, thought Kirsty.

"Let's hope he's to be trusted," someone whispered, an older, wiser maid with a hint of bitterness in her voice. "A sly fox o' a man, that one."

"The Queen's mother, Marie de Guise, trusted him," said her companion quietly. "She called him her true friend and loyal servant."

Kirsty watched the couple as they glided past. She saw no man present who so well-matched Mary of Scotland, no man she would more readily have trusted as her Queen's consort and co-ruler of the kingdom. She was disappointed when they disappeared from view, for even to watch them together brought a curious sense of pleasure and satisfaction, like finding by accident two perfectly matching gems.

While James Hepburn of Bothwell lived, she thought, the Queen would never lack loyal supporters, and yet even in that short measure, she knew too that some great sympathy and attraction existed between them. She shivered, wondering if the curtain of time had rolled back briefly in that moment, and she had been allowed a glimpse of destiny for two people who belonged together undeniably, for good or ill, for life – or for death.

Now the Queen emerged again, this time led forward by Lord George Gordon, the handsome heir of the Catholic Earl of Huntly. Watching them, hearing the Queen's laughter echoing to the gallery where she stood, Kirsty thought that even the mask she wore from convention rather than necessity, could not conceal her radiance, her brilliant smile.

And she wondered for the first time if the Queen felt lonely and resentful as she did herself, resentful of an unknown marriage not of her choosing, a marriage which she must undertake someday regardless of the desires of her heart. A Queen must marry not for love, but to provide an heir to the throne. From her little knowledge of the Queen of Scots, Kirsty was certain that she concealed the same passionate emotions as any young and unawakened girl, emotions which tore at the heartstrings of courtier, poet and peasant girl alike.

"I wish we could be down there among them," whispered one of the seamstresses.

"Not me, I'm 'feared – all those grand folk!"

"What about you, Kirsty, will you dare to come with me? All you need is a mask."

The idea was tempting. After all, this evening was once in a lifetime. She would never again attend the Queen's Revel.

They slipped down the stairs and tiptoed along the corridor where to their delight, two discarded masks lay upon a bench by a closed door. The giggles and a man's laughter from inside told their own story.

By the stair to the Long Gallery, Kirsty hesitated. "What about a costume?"

Her companion laughed. "That's neat enough, neater than most of the servants. Besides you will see plenty of miladies dressed up as country girls."

Once downstairs in the crowded gallery, Kirsty regretted her decision as her companion was immediately sought by an elegant French courtier. Kirsty was afraid of the great throng, afraid of being recognised by Dirk Farr or the Maries. She regretted leaving her fine vantage point in the gallery above, for here she could see nothing above the heads of the crowd. The heat engendered by candles and sweating bodies was oppressive, and she was glad to slip out of the open door on to the terrace. There on a stone seat in the arbour she breathed in the soft night air, watched over by a newly-risen firmament of bright stars.

If only, she thought, she had the man of her heart, for this was an evening for lovers. To be in love would bring the touch of paradise.

"May I have the honour of sharing your bench, mistress?"

She had not heard the man approach and turning, found herself staring up into the face of the Earl of Bothwell. Before she could reply he sat down beside her. " 'Tis hotter than hell in there, and more tiring than many a Border march."

"Like you not dancing, sir?"

His eyes raked over her appreciatively. "Nay, mistress, I prefer more private sports. Have you eaten yet?"

She shook her head. "I am not hungry, sir." Panic seized her. What if she encountered the Queen or the Maries at the supper table?

"Will you dance with me then? Perhaps we can stir some appetite in you."

Kirsty listened to the music drifting forth. " 'Tis a galliard – which I cannot dance."

He pulled her to her feet. "Nor can I, lass. But we can prance a few steps together."

"I saw you dancing with Her Majesty," Kirsty said accusingly.

He laughed. "Did you now? Does that somehow make me unfit for you?" As he looked towards the gallery his face was angry, and she guessed that the Queen had made other arrangements for her supper partner than to be escorted thence by the Earl of Bothwell.

Suddenly he laughed, throwing back his head and revealing fine strong teeth. "Follow me, lass, and you'll not put a foot wrong, I swear."

The heavy-lidded eyes mocked her as he added in a whisper, squeezing her arm. "At least not on the dancing floor. But later, who knows?"

"I would rather stay out here, sir, if it is all the same to you."

"Would you indeed?" His voice was eager. "Then we shall eat anon. Come." And taking her arm he led her swiftly back through the sconce-lit corridors, where a stone staircase descended into the courtyard. There were fewer lights, the shadows were deep and she observed nervously that they were occupied by lovers who dallied.

Lord Bothwell's hand no longer rested politely upon her elbow. His arm now encircled her shoulders, holding her hard against his side. She looked around in panic, wishing there was someone to whom she might appeal for help. She guessed at Lord Bothwell's reputation, and that taking some serving wench or any maid willing would be no more to him than the gratification of his other appetites at the court tables. She would be no more to him this night than if he should drink a goblet of wine, enjoying it, but her face and body soon forgotten.

"Nay, my lord," she said firmly as his lips sought hers. She had been reared to a strong moral sense by Grandfather Howison and the church told her of the hellfire waiting for fornicators. She discovered that Lord Bothwell was undeniably attractive and she shivered at his closeness. "Nay," she said again as he pressed her back into a shadowy alcove.

He was clearly surprised by her refusal.

"I know you not, sir. You are a stranger to me."

"A stranger, eh?" He laughed. "And what has that to do with a man and a woman but to make keener their pleasure? I assure you there is no better way for strangers than to become lovers."

"I have no desire for a lover. I am betrothed already," she added hastily.

"Is that so? Then why are you alone this night?"

Her back was against the stone wall and he leaned over her, one arm resting behind her head. "At least if we are not to dally, you will let me see your face." Before she could protest he had unclasped the mask. His face changed so rapidly that she wondered if her complexion had turned green.

"Your – Your – nay, by God's blood you are *not*—" He laughed. "But you are her very image." He pushed back the scarf binding Kirsty's hair and the blonde tresses tumbled down upon her shoulders. "God's love, mistress, this is a choice jest. Who in the devil's name are you?"

"Kirsty Howison of Braehead, at Cramond. My grandfather—"

He nodded slowly. "Aye, that explains it – I know of your grandfather and how the Queen's father showed such devotion for his rescue." His eyes glittered and Kirsty was more afraid than ever as he moved his body closer to her. Why did everyone make such a fuss about her likeness to the Queen? It was not of her choosing. She had no desire to look like the Queen when it caused such constant embarrassment.

"You surely know *what* you are, Mistress Howison," he said heavily, and seizing her face between strong hands, his lips sought and found hers, while she struggled to be free, her hands pressing hard against his shoulders.

"I bid you good evening, my lord Bothwell."

At the sound of that deep but chilly voice which she dreaded most to hear, Kirsty found herself free with the dark angry face of Dirk Farr staring down at her.

It was almost worse than being discovered by the Queen herself. As she looked at the two men who seemed ready to leap at each other's throats. She thought of the fight that would ensue, the scandal, and she groaned.

Why on earth had she ever let herself be persuaded to attend this Revel uninvited? And she had a sudden terrible vision of a man dead because of her, and another thrown into the deepest dungeon of the Tolbooth at the Queen's pleasure.

CHAPTER
NINE

THE situation in which the Earl of Bothwell found himself was one to which he was well accustomed and at this unexpected frustration of his plans, he showed no sign of being out of countenance.

Bowing to Dirk Farr, he smiled. "My lord Laverock, I bid you good evening. How do you fare this balmy summer?" They could have been meeting in the Ainslie Tavern, his voice was so cheery, his manner so genial.

"Well enough." Dirk Farr's voice was icy. "I see you have made the acquaintance of my betrothed." The word, the contemptuous glance in her direction, withered Kirsty to an unimportant fragment hardly worth the quarrel.

"Your betrothed? By God's blood, some men are born lucky," said Lord Bothwell, a hint of coarseness in his sudden laughter.

"And others have ill-luck thrust upon them, my lord." There was an unmistakable threat in Dirk Farr's tone and Kirsty glanced nervously at Lord Bothwell, whose hand flew to where his sword normally hung. Then again he laughed, shrugging off the dangerous moment.

"We merely pass an idle moment together." Turning to Kirsty, he bowed. "Mistress Howison, our short acquaintance has pleasured me greatly. Adieu."

He was gone and, shivering, Kirsty stared into the dark face which glowered sullenly into her own. "And who gave you permission to attend this Revel?" Dirk Farr demanded.

"No one. I came with some of the other maids. We watched from above and then decided to take a better look." Seeing his scowl, she added: "We do no harm, a Revel was hard to resist."

At her wistful tone he smiled. "Then do not let the Queen know." His sudden calm frightened her more than the rage she had expected, and he saw the sudden fear in her eyes. Smiling, he offered her his arm. "Since this is your first attendance at one of the Queen's Revels and I am off duty, let us at least enjoy it together. First we shall dance, then sup."

"Sir, I am not attired for a dance."

He did not seem to notice. "Gipsies cannot be choosers – so men say. Besides here none will notice, where milady mimics milkmaid!"

"Nay, sir, I would rather sup."

"And I would dance. You shall not refuse my request."

To her surprise he danced well, moving with the catlike grace of the gipsies, the ease of a duellist and a fighting man. Lulled by his sudden charm and graciousness, his lack of anger at her disobedience, Kirsty was also aware that they received admiring looks from the guests. The *Garde Ecossaise* wore no mask and at least Kirsty felt safe behind hers. She saw on the faces of the women that they found Dirk Farr an attractive man, and this new aspect also banished a little of the resentment which she had woven so carefully around him.

The dance over, he led her to the antechamber where the high-piled food was fast disappearing. Around the tables an intricate patter of attendants presented serving dishes of silver and pewter to each guest in order of rank. There was fish in great variety, cod, eels, pike, plaice, salmon and turbot, all cleverly disguised and garnished by the Queen's chef.

"Try the vendace," said Dirk Farr, recognising her bewilderment. "I can recommend it to you." It was delicious and new; she had never tasted this curious fish, part-salmon, part-herring, before. "The Queen introduced it to the court," he told her. "It comes only from Lochmaben, the hunting lodge of the Stuarts. In future you will recognise it by this." And he pointed to the curious mark shaped like a heart upon its head.

As well as fish they were offered game pie, cold roast veal

and wild fowls, and Kirsty decided that a quarter of the food being served that evening would have fed the whole of Edinburgh's more humble households for a year. She was, however, delighted with her first taste of the extravagant French sweets which Queen Mary had introduced: Candied fruits, fruits *en chemise*, chantilly and caramel baskets.

There was wine too, not drunk in the normal Scots fashion, but with comfits added after the French manner. These comfits, or *canards*, Dirk told her, helped to improve Scots wines, which were rough and immature by the French standard.

As he called for another goblet she recognised the improvement, but cared not to experiment with the Usquebaugh, the living water or whisky, so strong it made her eyes water and her throat burn.

"More sweet wine then," said Dirk and the attendant rushed forward. Dirk handed over their half-finished goblets, whose contents were carefully poured back into the original vessel.

Kirsty was marvelling at his capacity for food and drink when at last they followed the remaining diners into the gallery to watch the Queen again dance the galliard with Lord Bothwell.

"How well they look together," whispered Kirsty. She felt no resentment towards Lord Bothwell for their embarrassing encounter. He now had eyes and whispers for none but his beautiful Queen. It was obvious that he adored her, she thought, as she saw his admiration echoed upon every man's face, including Dirk Farr's. Even he, she thought, was in love with his lovely young Queen, whose height did nothing to detract from her softness and femininity, but merely added lustre to her beauty. Her radiant smile, her laughter encompassed all those present, from humblest page to noblest courtier. That, decided Kirsty, was the secret of true charm, for she made all those who entered her circle, no matter how briefly, feel cared for.

She looked around the gallery, and in the nobles who formed the rank of the Queen's admirers, there was no man a match for such a queen, other than the dangerously attractive James Hepburn, Earl of Bothwell.

Nay, there was one other, she had to admit grudgingly, following the covert glances of the women to the man at her side. Unhelmeted, in the splendid uniform of black velvet and silver facings, the scarlet of tartan sash and the bright *fleur-de-lys*, with his black hair, the single barbaric earring, the face with brilliant eyes and curved nose of a predator from some forest glade, he had the savage untamed look of a heroic warrior. A man who still carried the mark of another wilder forgotten race.

Aye, she thought, Dirk Farr, had he been born prince instead of gipsy, could have matched such a Queen as Mary Stuart. For he too had the quality of steel, of truth and shining courage upon which legends are built. If only he had not chosen her out of avarice, if only he had not humiliated her with the knowledge that as far as he was concerned he only wished to have her as wife because he believed her to be the Queen's half-sister! She saw on the faces of the women who looked in their direction that they too asked the same question. Why had he chosen the small, insignificant masked girl in her servant's dress?

"You are solemn," he whispered, and drew her close to his side.

"I do but think, my lord," she said. Confused, delighted, by the warmth of his arms about her waist. Could he read her thoughts? she wondered uneasily. This strange man could be anything, even a warlock, for he was like no other man in this gallery, nor perhaps in the whole of Edinburgh or the world beyond the Flodden Port.

" 'Tis pity the Queen cannot have my lord Bothwell for husband," she said as the pair danced past.

"That rough Border creature, so coarse and ill-bred?" said Dirk in a perfect imitation of Mary Fleming's voice, so that Kirsty laughed out loud. "Did you not know that he is newly wed to Lady Jean Gordon, the Earl of Huntly's daughter?"

Kirsty felt saddened by such news, disappointed beyond

measure that only a miracle could ever make him the Queen's husband.

As the dance ended, Dirk took her arm. "Fire and ice," he said. "Those two wedded would be the death of both – and all of Scotland will be the loser."

"Will?" echoed Kirsty. "But such a marriage can never be. You have told me he is wed already."

Dirk did not reply, but stared above her head out into the darkness as if he saw other shadows than the dancers or the trees moving against a starry firmament. "The Revel is over," he said and as the last candles were doused he took her arm. "Come, you shall take a cup of wine with me first, for I am in no mood to retire."

His tone was eager, light-hearted, his arm about her firm. Tonight he told himself he would brook no denial of his need for her. Her arm about his waist they walked swiftly across the courtyard past stables and armoury, while a jubilant Kirsty was also certain that while their relationship had struck a more harmonious note, the fresh air found her not quite steady upon her legs, a little dizzy from the heat and the wine. She stumbled, laughing, up a spiral stone stair and he opened the door into a small room, neat and tidy and masculine, with four military-style beds, also neat and without adornment.

"The quarters of the *Garde Ecossais* – I bid you welcome.' He bowed, laughing, and she stood by the door, suddenly shy at being alone with him.

A sweeping gesture indicated the contents of the room. "I share this humble abode with my fellow guards, but I do not expect their return until dawn, since the fortunes of love will keep them occupied elsewhere."

Rather unsteadily, she thought, he poured two goblets of wine. She seated herself nervously opposite him. He held up the wine in salute. "And what think you now of Holyroodhouse and of your Queen?"

"She is beautiful, a wise and gentle lady. And this is an evening I shall never forget," Kirsty answered.

"You might have had even more to remember," he

observed drily, "had I not arrived in time to rescue you from the clutches of my lord Bothwell."

"You are somewhat over-colourful in your description, sir. We did but talk. I was lonely—"

"Talk? Lonely? By God, is that how you interpret the scene. Mistress, I discovered you in his arms. In his *arms*." He sprang to his feet and the goblet spilled unheeded. He strode round the table, dragged her to her feet, all gentleness gone, his face flushed and ugly, inches from her own. "Since you are lonely and lust for hot kisses, then you shall have them. Aye, before God, you shall have kisses – and more than kisses, if that is what you pine for. But I shall choose the giver."

Too late she smelt the wine on his breath, and then her eyes closed and her senses reeled beneath his lips. Vividly she saw those other times, the first compassion, the second anger, the third in the game of Blind Man's Buff, ecstasy— And now here were kisses to bruise her mouth and destroy her soul. She thought she must die, she could not breathe, and yet deep within her something awoke and cried out for more of this sweet agony.

She felt his body hard against her own, and realised incredulously that he meant this to be her destiny – to be taken not in the silks and satins of a bridal bed, but upon a plain little cot – like an army whore.

As though impatient of the impediment of her garments, he began roughly unlacing, caressing her bare shoulders, her bosom. For a moment his touch brought Kirsty to the unbridled delight that had been her royal father's, but then she glimpsed the stern hard face above her, the line of thick black eyelashes hiding the crystal-clear eyes as he forced her back to the waiting bed. Panic engulfed her; she was sober Kirsty Howison of Braehead, granddaughter of stern Jock Howison and daughter of the Reformed Faith, of strong and upright morals. The man who held her was a gipsy, amoral, lecherous—

And then it was over. She heard stumbling footsteps outside the door, and a voice calling, and a moment later a young

man in the same familiar uniform swayed into the room. He
looked from one to the other, giggled, and then stumbled
over to one of the beds.

"I am for sleep," he chuckled drunkenly. "Nay, Dirk –
and you, lady, do not deprive us of your charming company.
I sleep heartily, do I not, Dirk? I promise I will not even
know of your presence—"

But Kirsty waited to hear no more. With sudden despera-
tion she tore herself from Dirk's slackened grasp and ran to
the door, the one glimpse she had had of his face robbing her
of any desire to look back. She did not wait to see if he
followed her but sped down the stairs and across the courtyard, refastening her gown as she ran. What was she to
think? He had saved her from the clutches of the Earl of
Bothwell, but did he believe that she had encouraged the
Earl's advances – that she had welcomed his by her accep-
tance of that quick, warm embrace of his in the antechamber,
or his arm about her shoulders as they crossed the courtyard
together?

Her guardian angel had been sorely overworked that evening, she thought with an hysterical little laugh. First in saving
her from Bothwell, and then from Dirk Farr . . . she would
lock the door of her bedchamber, and not tempt Satan
again!

But through the night she lay sleepless, remembering
Dirk's passionate kisses, his savagery that bruised not only
flesh but will. All her senses cried out against the loneliness of
the hours that crawled towards the day. For she saw that even
as she fled from him, she was already betrayed by the other
Kirsty, the dark creature who dwelt in the secret depths of
her being.

After a tormented, nightmarish sleep in which her dreams
presented Dirk Farr in the guise of lover or fiend, she awoke
early, afraid to face him as she walked to the Queen's apartments.

He was not on guard.

She did not know whether to be glad or sorry, having
composed and rejected a large number of suitably stinging

remarks to excuse what she now considered her wanton behaviour.

It was fortunate indeed that all thoughts of Dirk Farr were thrust out of her mind by the Queen's decision to leave almost immediately for Jedburgh to preside over the Court of Justice. On the day following, she delightedly announced that she would meet Elizabeth of England at a secret rendezvous.

In the frantic activity of the short time before the Queen's departure, Kirsty sewed from dawn until dusk, putting the neat delicate stitches into Her Majesty's gift of linen to her sister of England. Since Dirk Farr was heavily engaged with the Queen's plans, Kirsty was relieved that she did not have his presence to make her hands tremble, her fingers fumble at her sewing.

She found herself looking forward with eager anticipation to the end of this bustle of swarms of courtiers, maids, attendants, for ever racing up and down the corridors of Holyroodhouse.

"Her Majesty needs—"

"Her Majesty wishes—"

"Come at once."

Kirsty realised that her part was almost at an end. Although she was a little jealous of the Maries accompanying their Royal mistress, she also had come to realise that they were not altogether to be envied. In the past week she had observed that the Queen's moods no longer varied from day to day but from hour to hour. First hopeful, chattering excitedly, then doleful, ready to weep. Her *incognito* retinue would also include household grooms, lesser servants, her personal chef and assistant cooks, and as the day drew nearer, tempers in the royal household inevitably also grew shorter.

Aye, thought Kirsty, it would be a pleasant change to be out of the hustle and bustle, to have some time to spare. Away from Dirk Farr's eagle eye, perhaps she would manage to slip down to the Ainslie Tavern and regale her friend Rose with a catalogue of the events since she arrived at the palace.

At last the day of departure dawned, and from her bed-chamber Kirsty heard the palace astir with activity. Sighing happily she looked forward to going back to sleep. She had hardly closed her eyes when Mary Fleming was standing over her, shaking her gently.

"Awake, Howison, and get dressed – quickly!"

Fleming's urgency suggested some calamity, but even as Kirsty questioned her she said: "You are to come with us to the borders. Our Seton has taken ill. We expected her to return from her home last night. When she did not arrive, we were alarmed, but did not want to distress Her Majesty. This morning a messenger has ridden in to say that after nursing her brother through the New Influence, she has taken it herself."

Gentle delicate Seton had been summoned to Seton House to attend an ailing family and Kirsty thought of how disappointed Seton would be, how remorseful too, at not being able to accompany her Queen and the other Maries.

"Quickly, Howison," urged Fleming, taking down a cloak from the press and bundling together Kirsty's few garments. "There is much to do. 'Tis Her Majesty's command that you take Seton's place as maid-in-waiting, until Seton is able to resume her duties again. You may start at once!" she added as they hurried downstairs to the Queen's apartments. "Her Majesty has changed her mind regarding which gown she will wear for the meeting with the English Queen a dozen times this morning."

Kirsty found Queen Mary with Beaton and Livingstone preparing her for the journey, attiring her in the dove-grey velvet riding costume, while she darted questions at them as to whether her gifts for the English Queen were safely packed.

"Did you remember the ruby pendant? The pearl earrings?"

"Aye, madam."

"I do not recall seeing them."

"They are in the velvet casket."

Mary frowned biting her lip. "I am not sure that I put them in."

Exchanging an exhausted glance with Kirsty, Livingstone

unpacked the casket and presented it to Her Majesty, who was satisfied that the jewels had been included after all.

"And now, Howison, which gown shall I wear for the meeting? Show them to her, Beaton, for she has a good eye for colour. Shall it be the magenta velvet here?"

Kirsty examined it and thought that perhaps the slashings of orange satin and the wide billowing skirt might not travel well. The black velvet with its maroon underskirt and white lace veil, with its small coronet to hold the veil in place, she thought too regal, lending little to the pretence that this was an informal meeting between the two Queens. Finally she suggested timidly that the Geneva robe of claret, with its petticoat of a lighter shade might be most suitable.

" 'Tis most becoming to Your Majesty."

Mary beamed and clasped her hands. "I am glad you chose that one, Howison, for it has been in my mind that it would suit best. The skirt is less extravagant, so it will not spoil the day by becoming entangled with briars if we walk in the woods together."

"Might I suggest as an alternative, Your Majesty, the grey velvet you are wearing at this moment."

Mary frowned. "Nay, Howison, after several days in the saddle this would be inappropriate. Besides it is too masculine by far," she added firmly, meaning that it did not show off her curves to such advantage as the gowns she favoured.

At last they rode out of the palace, clattering across the drawbridge with every wood and tree around them serenading this retinue of cloaked travellers to birdsong, bright and glittering as the morn. But for the size of the retinue, the royal party might have passed for the merchants the Queen hoped to deceive passers-by into believing they were. Anonymous black hooded cloaks hid the finery of velvet and satin and the ladies were masked.

Kirsty heard the Queen's delighted chuckle, saw the gleam of her eyes. "Is this not fine play, *mes petites*, the grand adventure? No one will ever suspect that we are not some nobleman's family or some fine Edinburgh merchant moving from town house to summer residence."

Although the Maries agreed, their eyes were watchful. Kirsty knew too that the Queen deceived herself that this Border meeting of the two Queens was secret. She had heard whispers about the court that Queen Mary's meeting with Elizabeth was the gossip of every tavern and street-corner in Edinburgh. Tongues in Holyroodhouse's kitchens had wagged knowingly and the details of the Queen's destination after the Court of Justice at Jedburgh were freely discussed.

The Queen rode between Lord James and Lord Bothwell, and the faster beating of Kirsty's heart, the crimsoning of her cheek warned her that Dirk Farr had joined them. A travelling cloak hid his uniform and he was clearly surprised to see Kirsty in Mary Seton's place.

Now they rode briskly past the Nor' Loch with its seabirds and swans still asleep upon azure waters. The sun gleamed like a benediction upon the little cavalcade.

" 'Tis good to be alive on such a fine morn," sighed the Queen, "the air is like good wine."

Even Lord James smiled although Lord Bothwell replied dourly at his pleasure to be "away from Edinburgh pestilence and summer odours":

"God grant that we find no worse fate ahead of us."

A shadow fell at Kirsty's side, and Dirk Farr reined in beside her. "What do you here? I thought you were to remain at Holyrood until the Queen's return."

The day had cast its magic upon her. The Queen was right, this was a grand adventure. Why should Dirk Farr try to spoil it for her with his sour glances as she explained about Seton's illness?

"I would not have wished you to come. I was never consulted in this matter."

"Do you think, sir, that Her Majesty would ask *your* permission?" Seeing his expression she added: "I beg you, do not remind me once again that I am your property. Let me enjoy the honour of serving Her Majesty." He glowered at her and she sighed. "Oh, how can you be so dismal on a morning like this when all the world is joyous? Look at Her Majesty and learn from her – see how happy she is."

His smile was sad. "Gentle, trusting Kirsty, would for your sake that there were fewer villains in this little drama." When she exclaimed impatiently, he said grimly: "We shall see if Her Majesty is still happy when we ride back along this road – in safety, if God be willing."

His gloomy manner infuriated her, and she was glad when the road narrowed and she rode swiftly ahead and put some distance between them. Now they had reached the road which forked north to Cramond and Kirsty felt a sudden longing for what was now an almost forgotten home, an era of past life to which she could never return. As they crested the hill and turned south, she looked back over her shoulder and saw away in the distance the wide Firth of Forth, and beyond the sea, with its blue foam flecked in white, a flash of sail here and there, no larger than a mackerel's tail.

Far behind them crowded the tall houses of Edinburgh and the great castle riding the clouds. The corner turned, and the horses trotting briskly now, Kirsty realised that the journey, for good or ill, had really begun.

"Make way, make way there."

The bands of travellers whom they met were few and little interested in their passing cavalcade, all its royal insignia hidden under dark cloaks and hoods, with the litter in case the Queen should tire. At the moment such an idea seemed unlikely, since she was an excellent horsewoman who could outride all but Lord Bothwell. She rode with him in the lead, Lord James at their side, a few of Bothwell's servants concealing hagbut and axe under their discreet capes, since their master had insisted upon such precautions. In the centre were the three Maries and Kirsty, behind them the lesser servants. But close to the Queen's side, now that they had reached the open country, rode the four disguised *Garde Ecossais*.

Occasionally when they stopped, the Queen's laughter echoed back. The Maries exchanged delighted smiles of relief that the day had gone well so far. Like Kirsty, they had had moments of doubt that this journey would ever begin.

"Her Majesty is in excellent spirits," said Beaton.

"She is paler than usual," frowned Livingstone.

"I am fearful for her," whispered Fleming to Kirsty. "As we dressed her this morn, she sneezed thrice. But she insists that the New Influence would not dare threaten her meeting – not after so many prayers for its success!"

"Aye," said Livingstone overhearing, "Her Majesty has a will of iron and pretends that a healthy mind can rule over a weary body."

"Weary," yawned Beaton. "I thought we would never be quit of Holyrood. I slept but three hours before dawn."

On past the Queen's castle at Craigmillar, through twisting path and down leafy lane, past ancient abbey where monks working in the fields raised hands to foreheads, shielding eyes against the sun, and watched them pass. On through sleeping hamlets, up steep hill with a far glimpse of sea. At Crichton Castle, Lord Bothwell's by ancient right, they rested briefly, acquired extra mounts, were given refreshments and seen off with a stirrup-cup, while Kirsty marvelled again at their host's power, for they were in his land where he and his troopers were the law.

Leaving Crichton and climbing the hill of Soutra they entered a desolate land when the heather took over, and all around them the hills lay like sleeping giants and the sun crept over the still dark peaks turning bubbling streams first to blood, then to bright silver. With only tracks now through the heath, the sound of water was everywhere in bubbling burn and whispering under the squelch of hooves where treacherous bog gleamed emerald in the sunshine. The air was haunted by the lonely curlew's cry, and from a distant wood a cuckoo called.

Anxiously they regarded the sky, and for all the morn's bright beginning, Lord Bothwell swore that as a seasoned traveller in this land he could smell rain upon the wind. And Dirk Farr, a gipsy again, constantly scanned the horizon, alert to sights and sounds of which the others were unaware.

As for Kirsty, now that the first weariness had gone and she was used to being in the saddle, she felt exhilarated by the running breeze that whipped the hood from her hair, by the sharp smell of earth, the moss and sour bog water, the odour of sweating horses and polished leather. There was music in bird-call and jingling harness, in saddle's creak, and she pushed aside her mask and gave her face to sun and wind, soft as balm upon her cheek. Dirk, riding alongside, rested his hand briefly on her horse's mane and smiled. They were comrades now.

They went past the Eildon Hills rising three-coned from the soft green fields, with their stories of fairy-folk, their legends of travellers lured into Elfland and lost for ever. At last, beckoned by wooded valleys, they rode along the banks of Gala Water and into Galashiels where a crowd had gathered since it was market day. They lined the road through which the cavalcade trotted, cheering not the Queen whom they did not recognise, but Lord Bothwell, who acknowledged their greeting. Fresh horses were acquired and ale was brought forth. Kirsty watched him hold forth a goblet of wine to his Queen and pledge her with his eyes and lips.

The sun was hot now, and Kirsty was glad of the cool breeze, their swift movement as they skirted meadow and stream towards the towering grey ruins of Melrose Abbey where she hoped they were to rest that night. Hope was vain, for although the Abbot was half-brother to the Queen and Lord James Stuart, yet another of prolific King Jamie's illegitimate sons, Kirsty learned wearily that Jedburgh was their destination, and a house belonging to the Border Kerrs had been put at their disposal.

Unused to long hours riding over harsh moorland, saddle-sore and yearning for a soft bed, Kirsty was delighted to see far below them a huddle of grey stone with a twisting river gleaming like a silver ribbon in the early evening.

The Queen was expected in Jedburgh and the loyal citizens thronged the narrow street to bid her welcome. The cavalcade stopped before a stone house, corner-towered, almost hidden by an orchard, its ground deep in fallen blossom like a petal carpet, fragrant too. The house was small but hand-some and well-appointed, as was the chamber with a window overlooking the blue hills where the day's sun slowly set.

As they helped her disrobe, Queen Mary yawned, tired now but smiling still, watched over by the stern Biblical figures on the faded tapestries which lined the walls. They dined heartily upon simple fare, trout fresh-caught from the river beyond their windows, baked with herbs, and pro-ceeded by cock-a-leekie soup and bread, still hot from the oven, manchet bread made in the Queen's honour with the finest flour.

At the Queen's request Dirk joined them, sitting opposite Kirsty with the candlelight gleaming upon his strange face, whose features were more akin to those on the ancient tapes-tries adorning the walls behind him, than the faces of sixteenth-century Scotland.

From his cellar at Crichton Castle, Lord Bothwell had brought a vintage wine to furnish this intimate feast. He was comradely now towards Dirk Farr, and together they talked to the Queen of old campaigns in France,

Kirsty was glad to see them merry together, but drowsy with fatigue and wine, she lost the thread of their talk and was suddenly aware that the Queen was leaving. All jerked to their feet, bowing, curtseying.

"All is in readiness, madam, for the Court of Justice in the morn," said Bothwell.

As Kirsty made to follow the Queen with the Maries, she smiled and shook her head. "Nay, Howison, I need you not. Stay for a little while." And her smiling glance reached Dirk Farr, as if understanding the needs of lovers for time alone.

Bothwell departed cheerily, whistling under his breath, and Kirsty suspected that even in Jedburgh he had found an easy conquest.

Dirk laughed. "My lord Bothwell is ever able to match business with pleasure." He regarded Kirsty solemnly, held out his arm. "Will you walk with me?"

Kirsty yearned for rest; she was almost to tired to make the effort, but felt that she owed it to him, since tonight and on the march there had been new harmony between them. It was as if, away from the royal court, Dirk became a simpler, kinder man, one she might understand, whose roots were in the earth, in the things of nature, like her own.

She followed him out of the house and through the orchard to where the River Jed flowed under a hump-backed bridge. She leaned against its rail and stared down into the dark waters, too tired to talk.

They were both silent, and Kirsty glanced at him shyly. Tonight he had abandoned the brilliant uniform for the leather breeks and jerkin, the plain woollen shirt and thigh-boots of a Border soldier. Encountering his glance, Kirsty looked away, aware that these modest homely garments made him less forbidding than the stiff figure she encountered on guard outside the Queen's apartment. He ran a hand through his thick black hair, his pale eyes gleaming in the gathering dusk. "I like not steel bonnets," he said sighing. " 'Tis good to feel the wind in my hair." He laughed. "Although steel bonnets *are* useful in an argument."

Kirsty had heard the Maries whisper that they were glad the *Garde Ecossais* would be near, since they were acknowledged as fine soldiers and the best swordsmen in Scotland and France.

Dirk stretched his arms above his head as though to cast off weariness. He savoured the night with its first bright stars. He looked up at the window with its gleam of candle where the Queen and Lords James and Bothwell discussed the final arrangements.

"Are you afraid, Kirsty?" His voice was sharp.

"Nay, my lord."

"Then you should be, for in the meetings of great Queens lesser mortals – their feelings, desires, aye, their very loves – are of little import."

"What mean you by that, sir? The Queen loves us, cares deeply—"

"I mean Hermitage," he interrupted. "Hermitage tomorrow. And then the story that no history book will ever record. Until today only Elizabeth and her secretary, the Queen,

Master Armstrong and myself, knew the time and the place appointed." He stared back at the candelit square of the Queen's chamber as though he tried to listen through space and the thickness of stone to the conversation within.

He had never before referred to his part in the arrangements. Kirsty looked at him. The Queen must think highly indeed of this man to trust him before even the noblest in her kingdom. "What of this place where they meet?" she asked.

"A wood through which a stream flows, a footbridge across it, narrow but with enough room for two persons to meet. There our two Queens will kiss hands for the first time, as monarchs and as kin."

Kirsty smiled. How like Her Majesty to choose such a romantic place! As if Dirk read her expression, he shook his head.

"I like not this wood, for trees can conceal armed men."

"But the Queen will be accompanied." The Maries had indicated that they would be in constant attendance.

Dirk shook his head. "Nay, Elizabeth meets Mary alone."

"On a *bridge* over a *stream*?" exclaimed Kirsty. "Alone?"

"So you see the possibilities too, do you? Her Majesty assures us that the meeting-place was chosen with great care and forethought by Master Armstrong." His dislike of the man was evident from his voice. "He informed the Queen of the difficulties in persuading Elizabeth to a meeting within walls, since the English too are fearful of treachery." Seeing Kirsty's startled expression, he laughed. "Look not so, Kirsty. Elizabeth of England is a cultured, gentle lady and she is too near the wild Border land for her comfort. She has heard many tales, which alas are true. It is a land where knives in the back are not unknown," he added mockingly.

Kirsty now realised why the Queen was filled with such childlike excitement as the event drew nearer. These secret arrangements would appeal to her, even with the threat of danger, far more than any straightforward plan. She loved the need for disguise, danger added more zest to her passion for intrigue.

"We have all reminded Her Majesty that Elizabeth of

England is not trustworthy," Dirk continued, "we have
begged her to look to her safety, to her subjects' happiness,
by choosing Hermitage for the meeting – with my lord Bothwell's troopers at the ready in case of treachery."

He smiled at the memory of the Queen's delicate shudder
at this suggestion. "Her Majesty insisted that Hermitage is
not the most hospitable of dwellings and added, none too
tactfully, that my lord Bothwell's castle was such a fortress as
would terrify her dear sister of England. She said it was more
like a prison than a residence for a gentle Queen who was
used to elegance – and warmth."

"Where is Queen Elizabeth now?"

"Master Armstrong brought news that she is heading for
Keildar, and that he has spoken with her."

Again Kirsty noticed the sharpness of his voice. She was
surprised that he could allow personal feelings of animosity
to possess him at such a time. As if reading her thoughts, he
said:

"If I mislike the man, my reasons are sound. I trust him
not, despite Her Majesty's assurance. My Farrs have been
following the progress of the English right across the country
to Carlisle." He sighed heavily. "They have not yet received
word or any sign that the English Queen's retinue has left the
castle there."

"Surely you have told the Queen of this?"

He nodded. "Many times, but she ignores all pleas for
caution. If Elizabeth *appears* not to have left Carlisle Castle,
then this is part of her own devious plan, says her Majesty."
He smiled grimly. "The sweet lady is so certain that
Elizabeth is akin to herself, with a love of plot and counter-
plot, that she looks upon it as another bond in the forging."

Almost afraid to mention his name, Kirsty asked: "And
Master Armstrong, where is he?"

"He is at Hermitage, where we will all meet tomorrow."
He put out his hands like a blind man and touched her
shoulders. His hands tightened. "Lord Bothwell and I believe
that the Queen is too trusting. I am for Hermitage – and
beyond – this night, since we feel the situation is worthy of a

closer look." He did not press the point to Kirsty that the news from the Farrs, who had an excellent and reliable secret society on both sides of the Border, was disquieting. His gipsies were never wrong, but when he had told the Queen so, that he would trust them with her life, she had turned upon him in a fury saying that the Farrs might do well enough in loyalty, but did he expect her to take their word before that of her "dear sister of England"?

"You still believe that the Queen is in danger?" asked Kirsty in anxiety.

"Let us say I would like to contact my Farrs prior to the event." He was silent, staring into the darkness, and he no longer touched her. "Aye, Kirsty, when you have lived long as a soldier, when your life and that of your comrades depends upon being a step ahead of death, you learn to smell danger in the wind that blows. And before God, this very air is heavy with the smell of it."

"Howison? Are you there?" Fleming's voice from the orchard was urgent.

"I must go. We will meet again at Hermitage." She looked up into his face and how much she wanted that he should kiss her.

He was very still. "If I live, we will meet at Hermitage. But if I die, know that I love you – with all my heart." And with a little cry she went into his arms and felt his fast-beating heart, his kiss that held longing, despair. As Fleming called again and they parted with lingering hands, she yearned to call him back, for in his kisses she had tasted a lover's fear that this was farewell.

As she climbed the stairs behind Fleming, an owl called after her and she shuddered at this omen of disaster.

CHAPTER
TEN

KIRSTY had not long to wait in the matter of omens. The Court of Justice over, the Queen returned to the Kerrs' house lamenting a headache.

" 'Tis but weariness," she told the alarmed Maries. "A good night's rest, and tomorrow we will be at Hermitage." She clasped her hands together. "And the day after that, I shall stand face to face with my dear sister at last. Now naught can go wrong, for this morning we received a most loving message that Her Majesty rests at Bewcastle, and our meeting-place is arranged to the final detail."

The Queen retired early with a hot posset to relieve her aching throat, which, laughing shakily and unconvincingly, she put down to having talked more than usual that day during the court.

When Lord Bothwell heard that the Queen was slightly indisposed, he growled. "Talking never wearied Her Majesty's throat, nor did a Court of Justice set her head aching. I fear the outcome of this indisposition, ladies."

"Fear not, my lord," Livingstone said soothingly, "Her Majesty has a will of iron."

The Queen's coughing kept the Maries and Kirsty restlessly awake during that night. Next morning they were appalled by her flushed countenance, the dark rings about her eyes, as they took in her breakfast. Her shortness of breath declared the onset of fever, and the Maries begged her to return to bed.

"Your Majesty can delay the meeting by one day," pleaded Fleming.

"What? Keep my dear sister of England waiting, like some

common serving wench? You know not what you ask, Fleming – I had thought you knew me better, knew a Queen's word is never broken. I will go to our meeting even if I have to be carried there."

"But, madam—"

"Nay, argue no more, Fleming. My mind is set and you do but weary me further. *You* make me ill with such suggestions," she added shortly.

And so they left Jedburgh and its cheering crowd and rode through the summer morning along the banks of Rule Water, and by Windburgh Hill's small black-watered loch, secret enough to house the water-kelpie whom men claimed rose from its depths to claim a human bride. Through stream and shallow they rode and warily through green moss and wind-dragged heather. They reined in by the Allan Water, the horses' steaming in the sunlight, the noise of creaking harness outweighed by the broken cough which shuddered from the Queen's taut figure upon her white horse.

"Is it far still?" she croaked.

"Nay, madam, we will have you safe at Hermitage within the hour," said Lord Bothwell, his voice falsely cheery. "A good warm posset of Usquebaugh will put an end to your weariness."

On and on, to where the mighty heads of Greatmoor Hill and Cauldheugh stood blackly against a cumulous sky, heavy-clouded now, with only a blink of sunshine. There was no longer sign of habitation; this was a world where man had not yet been created, thought Kirsty, as they rode carefully through the dead heathland with its writhing skeletons of bare roots, where deep and sudden hollows cut into the hills by narrow streams marked the Border "beef tubs". Almost hidden from view by the steep slopes, they were the perfect natural hiding-places for stolen cattle. Riding was no longer brisk trotting but a careful picking one's way, following Lord Bothwell in single file along narrow paths, for without his guidance many a horse would have stumbled, its rider thrown, or all would have been lost in the bright treachery of emerald bog. Leading the Queen's bridle rein, he moved slowly through the wild terrain, and the only sound rivalling the wind's moan was her rasping cough.

"Hermitage, madam – see, over there."

"God be thanked, my lord." And the Queen swayed in the saddle. Lord Bothwell seized her, and the Maries urged their horses forward. Her eyes were closed and she looked like death itself, apart from the rasping moan of breath. "I will carry her. You follow in my tracks, carefully, my lord," he said to Lord James Stuart. "The others after us."

Descending to Hermitage Water, they came upon a circle of ancient stones that had been there since man's first remembrance. Aye, and long before that, thought Kirsty, with a shiver. So silent they stood, as if they had waited since the beginning of time for these travellers to appear across the moor.

" 'Tis a Druid circle," whispered Fleming, her voice awed.

"I hear tell that they made human sacrifices on those very stones," said Beaton.

"Aye, and they look at us as if they ken them still," said Kirsty glad to be riding past that evil place towards the huge granite fortress upon the banks of the stream. Proud, remote, inviolate, it incorporated into its walls something of the same power as Lord Bothwell himself.

As they rode nearer, Kirsty stared in awe at the main block. It was two hundred years old, the Maries told her, with those large square towers projecting at its four angles, the east and west towers linked by massive stone archways through which they followed Lord Bothwell and his royal burden into the cobbled courtyard.

Bothwell half-carried the Queen to her apartments, although she insisted that she was well able to walk. He left her reluctantly to her Maries and Kirsty, his heart in his eyes. Kirsty felt sympathy for his longing for this love he could never have for his own, although every other woman he touched could be his for the taking.

Dutifully the Queen drank, grimacing, the usquebaugh posset he sent her, although she refused to eat.

"I long to sleep only, that is what ails me." The cough was deeper now, as though it had settled deep in her chest. "Look not so sadly upon me, *mes petites*, I will be well tomorrow; remember I am in command of this body of mine."

Kirsty thought privately that the Queen's will of iron was no match for this "new influence", and her good spirits as they tucked her up in the vast bed were a pale pretence against a growing fever.

"A good night's sleep – you will see. Tomorrow at one in the afternoon we meet with my dear cousin a few miles away at the stream of Kershopefoot. The thought fills me with such joy and longing! I *must* be well, for I fear that not only the future of Scotland but a little of my own lies in the outcome of this meeting. Let us say our prayers and ask the good Lord to help us to a joyous day."

In their bedchamber which would have accommodated most of the rooms in the Kerrs' house in Jedburgh, Fleming said: "I mean no ill, ladies, but I think we should pray that Her Majesty of England is delayed until our Queen recovers."

Kirsty washed and put on a fresh petticoat before hurrying down to the Great Hall, anxious to see Dirk Farr. In the distance, a figure in *Garde Ecossaise* uniform hurried along the corridor and she rushed to greet him.

He turned round and disappointed, she saw it was not Dirk but his friend Harry, who she had encountered on the night of the Queen's Revel at Holyrood. Blushing at the memory, she asked: "I would speak with my lord Laverock, where is he?"

Harry frowned: "I know not, mistress. We expected to find him here already when we arrived at Hermitage. 'Tis strange."

"Did you know – aught of his destination?"

"Aye, mistress, he was to seek out Master Armstrong, some final details to discuss." The look which accompanied the remark suggested that she should have known that herself. Then, seeing her anxious face, he smiled. "I dare say there is naught for concern, these matters take time. He will have been delayed; perhaps Master Armstrong was not readily available."

Kirsty returned to the hall, where Lord Bothwell and Lord James had invited Fleming and Livingstone to sup with them. Beaton having elected to remain with the Queen, they insisted that Kirsty should join them. She did not greatly relish the supper hurriedly cooked from rather tough old beef and stale vegetables which even the Queen's chef could not make appetising, nor could he disguise its flavour with his variety of sauces.

Lord Bothwell put down her lack of appetite to anxiety over Dirk Farr's non-appearance, while Lord James frowned and looked angry, as if he disclaimed all personal responsibility in the matter.

As the meal progressed, Kirsty listened abstractedly to the conversation around her, alert for every footfall, and each time the door opened she expected to see Dirk stride across the floor.

The two Maries were yawning when at last the door opened and Beaton appeared. "The Queen wishes to see my lord Laverock."

"Tell Her Majesty he is not here," said Bothwell shortly.

Beaton looked at Kirsty. "Then where is he?"

Kirsty shook her head, and Bothwell said: "We know not. He should have been waiting here when we arrived." He sighed. "Even if he lost his horse or some misadventure befell him, he could have been here on foot by now."

As Kirsty followed the Maries up to their bedchamber, she was certain that something was wrong and that Bothwell was right, and some ill had befallen Dirk. Sleepless, she found herself going over their last conversation, remembering his strange expression, his parting words about death. She shivered. It was almost as if he had known he was not to see her again.

Just before midnight she heard a horseman ride in. Wondering if it was Dirk, she stole downstairs and found Lords Bothwell and James still seated at the table.

"You still say you do not trust him; why not?" Bothwell was asking.

"He is a gipsy, and such folk are well known to be unreliable, dishonest – and to have their price. I have never met a trustworthy one yet," said Lord James.

"So you think he might have been bought by Elizabeth of England to betray Her Majesty?" said Bothwell slowly.

"Worse than that – to sell us all, and Scotland too. Master Armstrong warned me against him."

Bothwell's fist thumped down upon the table. "Then why in God's name did you not warn the Queen?" he thundered.

"She would never listen, only repeat that she owed him her life. You know of her loyalty," he added scathingly.

"Had I known all this, my lord, then I would never have allowed him to go freely between the Scots and the English party. The scoundrel told me that he believed – aye, had certain evidence – that Master Armstrong meant to betray Her Majesty, and that there were five hundred English soldiers, armed, only half a mile behind the English Queen's so-innocent retinue."

"What of Farr's gipsies?"

"Loyal to Laverock – to a man." Bothwell sighed. "And I keep remembering the terrain that Elizabeth has chosen – with guidance, no doubt."

"You know the area?" Lord James demanded.

"I do, and I know that it would be perfect for an ambush. A bridge, a very narrow bridge, approached through a tree-lined gulley," he said grimly. "And whichever side Dirk Farr is on, the messenger I have just spoken to confirms that the troop of men on fast horses, riding far behind Elizabeth's retinue, had the tough look of fighters. For all their dark cloaks, he heard the chink of steel and thought that when the breeze blew they cursed, for it blew the cloaks aside and he saw the gleam of armour. This messenger of mine has eyes like an eagle, and I would trust him with my life."

Lord James stood up. "Come, we must awake Her Majesty." As Lord Bothwell began to protest, he was told

firmly, "The matter is too urgent for delay until morning."
Kirsty was so intent upon listening to every word that she
failed to realise she could not possibly escape unseen down
the long corridor as the two men rapidly approached.

"What do you here, Howison?" demanded Lord James,
seizing her arm. "Are you spying on us?"

"Nay, my lord, I did but hear a horseman approach and –
and I thought it to be my lord Laverock returning."

"Laverock, eh? We might have guessed that you would be
spying for him. Her Majesty will hear of this. You will
accompany us."

Lord Bothwell looked at her grimly. "Howison a spy? I
cannot believe it."

"I am not a spy!" Kirsty protested. "I love Her Majesty
and I would never harm her. Nor would lord Laverock. You
are wrong – wrong—" She began to cry as Lord James
dragged her by the arm towards the Queen's apartments.
What if the Queen refused to believe her?

Lord Bothwell put a restraining hand upon Lord James'
shoulder. "Gently, my lord. The child is but fearful for her
lover, her distress and curiosity are natural."

"Natural or not," snarled the Queen's half-brother, "she
comes with us and tells her story to Her Majesty."

The Queen thus wakened looked frail and ill, and while
Lord James put forward his accusations regarding Dirk Farr,
Kirsty forgot her own troubles and fears long enough to
observe the pain on Lord Bothwell's face as he looked upon
Her Majesty, knowing that he longed to take her in his arms
and shield her against whatever folly her trusting, noble heart
had led her to believe was for the good of her realm. She had
seen a similar expression on another man's face recently, and
remembered that thus had Dirk Farr looked at her the night
they stood in the Kerrs' garden at Jedburgh.

The Queen sighed and turned to Kirsty. "What say you to
this?" she asked gently. "Is Lord James correct in his
assumptions?"

"I am innocent, Your Majesty."

"And Lord Laverock? Is he innocent? Or have you knowledge that you are concealing from us, proof that he is a traitor?"

"Answer Her Majesty," roared Lord James, "or we shall wring the information from you."

Kirsty stared at him in horror, for she suspected that he might take gleeful delight in thumbscrew and rack if necessary. She shook her head. "I swear I am innocent. As for my lord Laverock, I know only that he loves Your Majesty, that he would willingly give his life to serve you, as I would myself." And unchecked the tears ran down her cheeks.

Wearily the Queen nodded. "Weep not, I believe you, *ma petite*."

"You are too trusting, madam," barked James, deprived of his prey. But, ignoring him, the Queen turned to Bothwell and asked:

"What say you in this matter?"

"From one of my own spies posted in the area, madam, I learn there are others at Keildar who have not yet set eyes upon the Queen of England. And Farr's gipsies seem to be busy about the area. Their camps are deserted. 'Tis a sure sign of trouble."

"Aye, madam," interrupted Lord James, "let us not forget their formidable numbers. In no time they could muster a sizeable army against you."

"Had they also arms with which to fight, swords, pistols? They could do little damages with staves," Bothwell reminded him that it was against the law for gipsies to carry arms.

"What think you, James?" said the Queen.

"I think that there is little cause for alarm, but perhaps a little for caution," he said smoothly. "Lord Bothwell is, I fear, being over-anxious, for I have every reason to believe that the litter borne from Keildar towards our rendezvous contains the person of the Queen of England."

"Then why does she not ride?" demanded Bothwell. "For I also have it upon the authority of mine own eyes that she is an excellent horsewoman, equal to Your Majesty."

"The reason is not hard to find," said Lord James.

"Doubtless she fears recognition, or is wearied by her travels. The road is long from London to York, then to Hexhamshire, Carlisle and thence to Keildar." To the Queen he continued: "Your fears are groundless, madam. Take heart. A few hours hence and you will be face to face with your royal cousin. This time tomorrow, God willing, we will be returning to Edinburgh."

Queen Mary frowned. "I would be happier if I could see my lord Laverock. Where *is* he? He promised to be here to await us."

Lord James and Bothwell exchanged glances but said nothing.

The Queen stretched out a hand to Kirsty. "Poor Howison, try not to fret. I am sure there is some good reason for the delay."

A good reason, thought Kirsty later, lying sleepless in the dark, trying not to imagine Dirk lying dead in a ditch with a knife between his shoulder-blades. The hours before dawn seemed endless, the castle was cold and gloomy even in summer, and every sound disturbed her. A wind arose, and in the patter of rain doors rattled like the clatter of swords, the heavy shower was the marching of an approaching army. At every new sound Kirsty sat up in bed.

Why did he not return? She heard riders in the night, longed to race down to the courtyard, but she restrained her impulses, wishing for no further encounters with Lord James, no raising of his suspicions.

She told herself: be calm. Even if Dirk did arrive, he could hardly let her know until morning, especially as she shared a bedchamber with the Maries. At last, exhausted by fears and misery, she fell into a slumber of sorts and it seemed that she had hardly closed her eyes before Fleming shook her by the arm.

"Has Lord Laverock returned?" she asked at once.

"I know not, Howison, I have just awakened. Hurry now, for we are to attend the Queen."

Kirsty helped the Maries dress the Queen warmly for her ride to the rendezvous at Kershopefoot. She pouted at their care of her, saying that such garments were ugly and deserved December rather than June.

The Maries exchanged glances and avoided looking at the windows for fear of depressing her further. The traditional "Queen's weather" had returned in full force. Rain had fallen heavily during the night, turning into a steady drizzle, and a Scotch mist covered the moors around Hermitage with an eldritch wind turning the summer leaves inside out. The Queen was seized by another bout of coughing and, refusing their assistance, she choked helplessly, murmuring, "It will pass. It is naught." The Maries looked at Kirsty, and she saw written in their eyes that the Queen could never accomplish one mile of the journey before them on horseback in such weather.

She refused all food, but drank a warm posset which she swallowed with difficulty. Sweating and shivering alternately, weak with fever, her limbs shaking, she staggered from her bed to collapse weakly into a chair by the fire which had been lit for her.

She knew she was beaten and even as the Maries added their protests to the folly of venturing out of doors, in such weather and so ill, she held up her hand and nodded weakly.

"Send for Lord James, if you please,'" she croaked.

Lord Bothwell came instead, saying that Lord James was involved in final arrangements for the journey. He gave Kirsty a sour look. "And there is no sign yet of Dirk Farr," he added, as if she was somehow responsible for his non-appearance.

"What shall I do, my lord, what shall I do?" And the Queen began to cry, her tears not only of misery but of frustration for all her efforts for this meeting being brought to such a sorry end.

Bothwell patted her hand like a sick child's and whispered, "Your Majesty cannot make this journey. It would be folly for which your own death would be payment."

"I know – I know! But I must go. 'Tis not for personal vanity, that you understand, but for Scotland's sake. I will go. Come, my Maries, we have wasted enough time."

Gently Bothwell pushed her back into her chair. "I say you will not go, madam. For Scotland's sake, for your loving subjects, you will remain here at Hermitage until you are recovered. We will get a message to Her Majesty of England, explain what has happened. Perhaps she can be persuaded, since you tell us she loves you well, to take pity and come to Hermitage."

The Maries exchanged glances. Even they thought Bothwell's suggestion naïve, since not only was Hermitage unfit to receive a great Queen like Mary, but would be out of the question for Elizabeth of England too.

"She would never come, my lord," said Mary, "she would suspect a trap. And who could blame her?"

Kirsty decide that one glance at Hermitage's grim walls would dissuade anyone of a nervous disposition. With its frightening reputation, even the strongest would tread warily.

"Your country needs you alive," Bothwell continued, "you cannot be allowed to throw away your own life and Scotland's future, the well-being and happiness of your loyal subjects, on this meeting. How then would your desires be accomplished? I am an old soldier, madam, and I have a strange awareness of danger, a feeling I cannot shake off, for it is like an ague in my bones."

Kirsty looked at him sharply as his words brought back with utmost poignancy Dirk's own sentiments which he had expressed before leaving Hermitage. Never to return? prompted her ready imagination. She closed her eyes for a moment against the Queen's woes, and prayed that he was safe. If only he would walk in that door, even scowling at her, she would admit that she loved him, she would run to his arms.

"God Almighty, madam, trust me!" Bothwell went down on his knees before the Queen, staring into her pale face, seizing her hand in his. "I have only your Majesty's safety and that of your realm at heart. You know well that I was always against this piece of folly."

"Only because Lord James was in favour of the meeting,"

said the Queen, with a little of her old spirit. "Will you two never agree upon anything? Must you be always at logger-heads?"

"Madam," said Bothwell slowly, "If 'twere simple as that, I would lie down upon the ground here at your feet and allow Lord James to trample upon me. Gladly, madam, a thousand times, if you would but abandon this meeting."

"If only my lord Laverock had kept his promise! If only he had brought the news he promised," sobbed the Queen. Her tears were unrestrained, and she was too weak to withstand Bothwell's anger or to fight him.

"We cannot hold your decision any longer. We must leave within the hour, with or without my lord Laverock," said Bothwell, for once the Queen's tears were lost on him. "And I beg of you – I *beg* – that you remain here. For who knows if the English Queen has kept *her* word? If Laverock spoke true, and even my spies reported some gey strange happenings in the area, none has seen inside the litter purporting to carry Elizabeth. What if it carries an impostor, someone whom at a distance bears sufficient resemblance to the Queen, to deceive the onlookers?"

Mary gave a little gasp. The Maries and Bothwell all turned slowly to stare at Kirsty, as if they had been struck with one identical thought. Bothwell crashed his fists together and throwing back his head, his roar of triumphant laughter filled the room.

"The play-actress – by all that is holy, we have her here! And a part made for her."

While Kirsty stared in astonishment, he strode across and seized her hands: "Will you do this, lass? For your Queen and for Scotland?" He remembered Mary's presence, cleared his throat and bowed: "With your permission, madam."

Mary clasped her hands together and closed her eyes. "It is the dear Lord's answer to our prayers. By His will Seton could not be with us and Howison, who is my double, took her place. Jesu be thanked." As she bowed her head, Both-well said to Kirsty:

"There may be danger in this, for all of us. 'Tis a bold and daring thing to deceive the English Queen, but there is no other way. Only you, Howison, can save your Queen. Will you do it?"

Kirsty's lips trembled. "I am fearful, my lord, I like not pretending to be Her Majesty – and before the English Queen—"

Bothwell seized her hands. "Lass, if your sire was whom we know him to be, then you have the royal Stuart blood, the courage and the daring that goes with it," he added in a whisper.

Kirsty looked at the sorry scene before her. Even if Bothwell could resist the Queen of Scots' tears, then she could not. Even if her own heart ached with anxiety and remorse over Dirk's strange disappearance, she knew clearly where duty lay. In that moment of decision, her grandfather – and her royal sire – would have been proud of her.

"I will do it, an it please Your Majesty," said Kirsty curtseying to the Queen. "But I fear I will never deceive Her Majesty of England. She is sure to know as soon as I speak, or walk towards her, that I am not Mary of Scotland."

"Not on horseback, seen from afar," said Bothwell triumphantly. "As long as you remain seated, with your mouth closed, then you could deceive anyone. Even Lord Laverock was deceived, remember that, madam."

There was a moment's stunned silence while they brooded upon the audacity of such an imposture. The Queen held out her hand.

"I have a plan which might work. Howison shall ride out with us, upon my horse, to be seen at a distance by the English party. Elizabeth will know that I have kept my side of the bargain."

Bothwell sighed. "Then I shall find means of reaching Elizabeth, and explaining to her what has happened. I will try to persuade her to come to Hermitage," he added with a smirk, "for I found favour with her, which she might remember."

"Nay, my lord," the Queen rose somewhat unsteadily to

her feet, "I will not remain here at Hermitage and you will not command *me*. I shall go to Kershopefoot as planned."

"But, madam—"

"It is my will and I will have it in this matter. Do you not see, my lord, that whatever you do Elizabeth will suspect a trap, and it would be worse than ever if she knew that an *impostor* was being paraded as myself."

While Bothwell gnawed at his lip and scowled, she continued, "Hear my plan. I shall accompany you in the litter. I shall not take further ill, for I am already well-wrapped for a Scottish winter, let alone a summer's day. I assure you, my lord, that I shall be as warm and snug in my litter as ever I was in this bedchamber," she added reproachfully. But her eyes were shining. "Howison shall ride my horse, as my lord Bothwell suggests, and I shall be carried in the litter until we are in sight of our destination. We will let the English see Howison, then she shall ride back, and exchanging cloaks with me, she shall take my place in the litter concealed from sight." She paused, took a deep breath. "With Lord James as escort, I shall walk the short distance to the bridge and have my meeting with Elizabeth as we have arranged."

"You cannot do it, madam," said Bothwell.

She turned to him. "Can I not, my lord? Then watch me." She extended her hands to all of them, beaming like a happy, excited child. Here was another grand adventure, more dangerous and daring than her original plan. Another chance for the disguise and intrigue that were her second nature.

"Come, my Maries, we have wasted enough time. Let us depart while we are in good spirits."

"But, madam," began Bothwell helplessly.

"Enough, my lord. My mind is made up, there is no more to be said. Come, *mes petites*, put Howison into one of my robes, and my best wig too."

Kirsty placed herself in the maids' hands, her blonde hair hidden by the peruke, a velvet gown with white ruff about her neck. A velvet bonnet and white veil completed the picture.

While the Maries assured her that although the velvet

cloak, which was much too long, trailed the floor, it would not have the same disadvantage upon horseback, a sound at the door had Kirsty turning quickly to see the newcomer, her heart fast-beating.

It was not Dirk. Lord James had arrived, and without looking in his half-sister's direction, he bowed to Kirsty. "My apologies for being tardy, madam, there was much to do—"

Mary's chuckle from the shadows had him spinning round. He stared at Kirsty and whispered: "In God's name, madam, what folly is this?"

As Mary breathlessly outlined the plan, croaking and coughing as she did so, it was evident even to Lord James that she was too ill to make the journey. However, he looked increasingly glum and even Bothwell's smile lacked conviction.

" 'Tis greatly to be desired, madam, that all will go as your Majesty hopes and plans," he said at last.

It was midday when they at last stared down over open moorland to a stream winding its way into a small wood.

"On one side of that water we are in Scotland. When we cross to the other side we are in England," said Bothwell.

So that was why this meeting-place had been chosen, the perfect spot for an incognito encounter between the two Queens. Kirsty surveyed the scene from the hilltop. Quiet, secluded, but it also had the advantage of being open country. Not a tree or bush marred the expanse of heath and moorland until they reached the stream's tree-lined banks far below. A place of safety, they had told themselves when they saw the plan which Master Armstrong had brought, a place almost impossible for ambush. So they had been assured.

Everyone now concentrated attention on the trees, still some distance away, which concealed within them the wooden bridge. Kirsty saw that the track, leading gently downhill, narrowed before disappearing into the trees. All was silent, only the restive horses, the chink of stirrups, broke the great summer peace of insects humming all around them. The drizzle had ceased as they left Hermitage. The mist had vanished and a weak sun strove for life.

They were aware of another sound, that of the distant stream, and its voice was greater than any herald's fanfare in Queen Mary's ears. For this was journey's end. Her face, pale and exhausted, peered at them through the curtains.

From the other side of the hill a horn sounded, once and again.

"There they are, madam."

And Kirsty saw a group of horsemen with a litter in their midst emerge from the opposite hilltop and begin the descent towards the wood. As Kirsty, seated on the Queen's white horse, moved forward, the English party recognised the Queen of Scots and a distant cheer arose, a waving of bonnets. For one dazzling moment, uncertainty vanished and pride took its place. She was no longer afraid that the venture would fail, and holding her reins proudly, head held high, she acknowledged their greeting. Kirsty Howison was in that instant, for the first and last time in her life, the "little princess" her grandfather had loved. In every fibre of her being she *was* Queen Mary of Scotland.

"Well done, Howison," whispered the Queen. A bout of coughing seized her and Kirsty saw Bothwell anxiously pour out a posset and her hand stretched out for it. He looked across at Kirsty.

"Out of sight there is a wooden bridge, narrow but wide enough for two people to stand upon it and talk in private." He looked at the English party. "See, they make speed, but have further to travel than ourselves."

Mary moved the curtain aside. "That is to our advantage. For once we reach the shelter of the trees, I will walk the remaining distance to converse with my cousin. Aye, James," she added to her half-brother, "even if you must carry me to her, wrapped in furs, I will not be thwarted."

As she spoke, the sun blazed forth upon them and the little group was bathed in its warmth. The Queen lifted her head, closing her eyes. "A sign, my lords. Even the weather is on our side like God's blessing."

All misgivings set aside, they descended the hill and rode across a clearing sparkled gold by early broom. They saw that the track through the little wood was narrow indeed and lined with flowering hawthorns. The stream's murmur was loud now.

"We cannot take the litter any further," observed Bothwell grimly.

The Queen sighed. "Is it far to walk? Where is the bridge?"

Lords James and Bothwell walked a few paces into the wood and returned. "It must be some distance still, for it is not clearly visible."

Lord James bowed. "I will take Howison until the bridge is in sight. When we know how far it is for you to walk, we will return and you can take Howison's place as you intended. Surely Her Majesty of England will not object to you riding instead of walking, when you explain how ill you have been?"

The Queen frowned. "Is it possible to see the bridge without being seen?"

"Aye, madam," said Bothwell. He sounded reluctant, thought Kirsty.

"Very well. Go with Lord James, Howison, but take care not to be seen. Then ride back to me, and if I feel strong enough I *will* walk, whatever my Lord James advises."

Lord James' face was expressionless as he led Kirsty still disguised as the Queen along the narrow sun-dappled track. Her horse's hooves stirred up a carpet of last year's fallen leaves, and at their acrid smell of decay, Kirsty shivered. The smell of death, she thought, and suddenly wondered why everything that was happening, and the dread that filled her, felt like an experience she had lived over and over. "*Déjà vu*" the Queen had called it and Kirsty fought back the terror that gripped her as she remembered that she was not completely a play-actress, for she carried in her veins the same blood as those ill-fated Stuart kings, prone to sudden death by violence.

The track seemed endless. She glanced back over her

shoulder, but Bothwell and the royal litter were out of sight now. Lord James was striding ahead, holding the horse's leading rein. She stared over his shoulder, her scalp prickling with fear, telling her that something was wrong; something indefinable, terrible, unseen. Then she realised that the birdsong which had so lushly filled the air moments ago had ceased. The path before them was too still, silent and yet menacing. She was certain she saw movement in the trees from the corner of her eyes, and felt as though a thousand eyes malevolently watched from behind every bush.

Would the bridge never appear? Would Lord James never give the order to return for the Queen, to exchange cloaks with her, to take her place?

A moment later, Lord James pointed ahead. "Look!"

And there was the bridge. Empty, sun-dappled with an innocent air of waiting. A simple rustic bridge over a stream. Her imagination had played her false, Kirsty thought, sighing with relief, for there was no sign of treachery, no justification for the terror within her.

Lord James was still walking ahead moving in a circle and turning her horse's head. But he still did not give the order to return. Suddenly he stumbled on some hidden object in the carpet of leaves. He gave a cry and Kirsty saw him sprawl helplessly, cursing on the leaf-covered ground which had broken his fall. Her horse whinnied softly as though scenting danger, and as Lord James struggled to his feet the scene turned away from a peaceful summer day into a terrible nightmare from which there is no awakening.

From behind every bush and tree, there erupted a great ragged grim-faced army. Their leader, wrapped in a cloak whose deep hood hid his face, seized her bridle and even as she screamed, she saw his followers restraining Lord James from escaping.

"You are in deadly danger, madam!"

Her captor rode swiftly ahead, leading her horse towards the rustic bridge over the stream which was Scotland on one side and England on the other.

Kirsty felt as though her heart would break, for she had no

difficulty in recognising Dirk Farr's voice. Even though the hood gave anonymity, she glimpsed black hair, the glint of an earring, the eyes that were pale and crystal-clear.

Too late she realised why he had not returned to Hermitage. He had never intended to do so. Lord James had been right: Dirk Farr was a traitor, a spy in England's pay.

CHAPTER
ELEVEN

"Trust me, madam," he said.

How could she trust him? Kirsty made a last bid for freedom as they approached the bridge. Leaning forward, she tried to wrest her horse's reins from his grasp. He had not expected this assault and the movement of prising her hands loose revealed that under the cloak he wore a dark crimson doublet.

"There is no time to explain, madam."

Explain, she thought, why he had discarded the uniform of the Queen's *Garde Ecossaise* and with it the loyalty to his mistress as he abducted the girl he believed to be the Queen of Scots, and delivered her into the hands of England?

England. They were in England now, for the bridge was behind them. At any moment now the soldiers would appear, and taking her from him hand over to this other Judas a bag of gold.

But instead of racing up the hilly slope as she expected, Dirk plunged down towards the stream's bed, leading her horse. There through the dappled shadows they galloped swiftly, followed at a distance by horsemen who were obviously Farr's gipsies. Why the water, thought Kirsty, and then remembered that it would obliterate all possibility of pursuit.

Dirk held fast to her reins. Above the stream's incessant murmur, she heard the alert sounded by the call of hunting-horn. Carefully now they rode through heavier undergrowth, avoiding the overhanging boughs which threatened to unseat them.

Bitterly, Kirsty stared at her captor's broad shoulders. Near to tears, she remembered how he had beguiled her into losing her heart to him with warm kisses, tender embraces, a lover's lips. Bitterly too, she remembered Lord James' warning, Master Armstrong's warning. They had been right, she had been wrong. They had watched her give her innocent heart and, experienced in detecting treachery, had known the outcome full well. Small wonder they had suspected her of being in league with Dirk Farr, for they had also known how easily a simple girl could be seduced from the truth by a clever rogue.

She looked at him again. Sometimes he slumped a little in the saddle as though weary; at one time the movement would have made her long to comfort him. What, she thought, had turned him traitor, what single act had changed him from the path of devotion not only in Scotland, but in France also, to Queen Mary? Apart from his hatred and distrust of the Gorgios, as the Farrs called all non-gipsies, she could think of no reason except reward. But what did he need? for he had the lairdship of Laverock, and the respectability such a title brought him in the world's eyes. What temptation had been strong enough to buy him for the English Queen?

Looking at his now weary shoulders, she remembered that only a short while, mere hours ago, she had feared for his safety, feared that his non-arrival at Hermitage heralded some ill which had befallen him. At this moment it would have been better for all, herself included, had her worst fears been true and Dirk Farr of Laverock lain dead in a ditch.

She must warn the Queen, she thought.

But how? Escape seemed impossible, even if she managed briefly to evade this experienced band of Farrs who now followed them closely, she could never hope to retain her freedom for long in this treacherous land with its hazards of mist and bog.

As though aware that escape was in her mind, Dirk Farr turned in his saddle and inclined his head toward her. "Take heart, Your Majesty." And he grinned, the ghost of his old self.

Your Majesty. And suddenly Kirsty realised that she might still outwit him, since he was ignorant that he had not

captured the Queen. She thanked God that the pretty velvet
mask, which convention and summer sun demanded, still
screened most of her face. Whatever happened to Kirsty
Howison, Queen Mary was safe and at this moment, she
hoped, being carried swiftly in the litter, back to Hermitage.

Kirsty blessed the good fortune by which the Queen, that
very first day in Holyrood, had sworn her to secrecy regarding her imposture, swearing her to keep it secret even from
Dirk Farr. With relief she remembered that although he had
once seen her in the role of Queen Mary, he had not the
slightest inkling that it was not the Queen herself he saw.
Now she knew that the longer she could maintain the fiction
that she was Queen Mary, the longer their royal mistress
would have to reach the safety of Hermitage, summon an
army to protect herself.

As for Kirsty Howison, how could she deceive the English
once Dirk handed her over to them. It could certainly not be
for long, but perhaps she could gain a little time if none were
certain of the Scots' Queen's extra inches. Kirsty would have
to keep silent though since her play-acting did not include
mimicry and it would have been impossible for her to imitate
the Queen's cultured tones, with the faint French accent.

Masked and on horseback, she could fool her captors. On
the ground she might take refuge in a pretence of having lost
her voice, or refuse to speak, hoping to have her action
mistaken as righteous anger and contempt. However, if Dirk
Farr had opportunity to examine her face more closely, he
would soon realise from their late intimacy that he had been
tricked. A lover knows each eyelash, each glance, each dim-
pled smile. To those who had seen her distantly as the Queen
she had been but an effigy, not a woman of flesh and blood.

As from every dark shadow another figure slipped out to
join Dirk Farr's ragged army, she realised any hope of escape
was forlorn indeed.

How long before they reach their destination with the
English?

At a clearing a man came forward, leading fresh horses.
How well Dirk Farr had planned it all, she thought, even to

the smallest detail, as a great black-visaged giant of a man with the look of a blacksmith came forward and, bowing, indicated that she take a fresh horse.

Dirk was watching her, leaning over his horse's neck. How strained he looked – for the hood had fallen back and there was no longer need for disguise. His face was ashen, his eyes dark hollows. She realised he must have ridden far and slept little to look so.

"Madam," he said, "if you will."

She shook her head furiously thrust her chin into the air and turned her face from him.

"Your Majesty's horse is useless for riding over difficult country. With your permission, madam." He nodded curtly towards the blacksmith who strode forward and transferred her bodily in one swift movement, as if she weighed no more than a sack of oats, on to the smaller, faster horse. She dared not struggle for fear she might dislodge her auburn wig, and once on the horse's back resisted the temptation to raise her hands to her hair.

"Do not fear, Your Majesty, you are safe with us. Your own horse will be returned to Hermitage. Saul here," he indicated the grinning giant, "will keep your leading-rein, for the paths are dangerous through the marsh lands."

If she could have escaped Dirk she had no chance of eluding Saul, who could have carried both her and her new horse on his back if need arose, Kirsty thought. Bitterly she stared at Dirk, wanting to cry out reproaches upon him, demand in a dozen questions why he had betrayed his Queen. But she bit back curiosity; she must remain silent at all costs. Until they reached the English, every moment gained by her meant safety for the Queen.

Her smaller swift Border horse had little difficulty in keeping pace with the horsemen who stopped upon a hilltop and stared back the way they had come. Intently they listened, and as if satisfied that they had eluded pursuit, Dirk Farr indicated that they proceed.

As long as there was sunlight, Kirsty could estimate the passing of time by the shadows lengthening over the land, but as heavy mist closed in on them again time itself vanished with the landscape. The path twisted and turned so frequently that she lost all hope of remembering direction, even had she been able to escape.

Resolved to retain her pretence of being the Queen until she was eventually unmasked when Dirk handed her over to the English, Kirsty found her thoughts beating back and forward, like a rat trapped in a cage. All those dread events which had led to this day from the innocent May morning when grandfather had taken her to Edinburgh and she had believed that Andrew Gledstane was to be her husband.

But Grandfather had died, Andrew had chosen a rich wife and Uncle Wat, as her guardian, had sold her to Dirk Farr. If only Grandfather had been persuaded to stay at Cramond, ill as he was, she would not be in this dire peril, but preserving summer fruits in the kitchen at Braehead. The thought was frightening, but ironic enough to make her smile wryly.

It had all begun in Edinburgh at the May Day Fair, for if she had not met Dirk Farr he would not have struck his "bargain" with Uncle Wat when Grandfather died. If she had not closely resembled Queen Mary, Dirk Farr might not have wanted her at all. He had admitted that his gipsy sense of acquisition had prompted him to acquire the Queen's half-sister, and with her the added dignity of royal blood, however bastard, to the Clan Farr.

If she had not been ill-used, lost and lonely and needing comfort, she might not have turned to him for comfort and discovered that need was also the beginnings of love.

If – if – if, jingled the horse's harness.

If—

Such thoughts were vain, too late to change the vagaries of the human heart. And she had lost hers to a traitor, a foolish action with which she was likely to pay, one way or another, with her own life. At that moment, her future had too little substance for her to care what became of her, mending and re-building her broken life once more.

They had rejoined the stream and now trotted along the water's edge as Dirk Farr searched for a crossing place. For a moment he slumped forward and seemed to lose his stirrups, one of the men rode over and there was a moment's anxious consultation as Dirk put his hand to his side and shook his head. As he straightened his back with effort, Kirsty wondered if he had been wounded in some fight before they met.

She considered him as they rode into a copse of trees which emerged as a drover's road across the hills. If he was like to die, then she might escape from the Farrs. But the thought of his dying, of that strange alien face, so beautiful to her now, being stilled for ever and the light growing dark in those crystal-clear eyes, brought no pleasure, only the pricking of tears to betray her further. Her heart was not yet used to his villainy, her body still yearned for him, loved him still.

If he had ridden this distance wounded, then he must be in agony, weak with loss of blood, she thought. No man could have such endurance. And she tried to comfort herself with the notion that he was but tired, and wondered instead where and when he had last slept.

The terrain ahead was rock-strewn and patches of bright emerald indicated bogs in which a man and horse could disappear without trace. There was no longer any idea in her mind that she might try to escape as they made a stumbling, tortuous progress up hill and down dale. The heavy mist descended again and she was soon chilled to the bone. It was all she could do to keep her tired, aching body on her horse, by holding tight to the saddle-horn and letting the animal, which knew the country a lot better than herself, find its own way.

At one stage she began to cough, swaying with weariness. Immediately Dirk Farr was at her side, his face deathly pale, his eyes burning against the blackness of eyebrows, the sooty density of eyelashes.

"Your Majesty, I apologise, but we will soon have you safe."

"Safe?" She allowed her lips to frame the word.

"Aye, madam, you will be safer at Laverock than at Hermitage. There was a plot to kidnap you," he said grimly, and gently touched her gloved hand. "Trust me, madam."

Laverock was at least Scotland still, and there were trees around them instead of the stricken stumps, weather-beaten and twisted by a long battle with the elements. The mist rose as they descended from the high ground and she saw across the grim valley, nestling between bosomy hills, a tiny castle with houses and a church tower.

The sight brought new heart to the travellers and the gipsies now ran lightly alongside, leading their horses. Agile, fleet of foot, she saw how such a band of men could carry messages the length and breadth of the land. They needed no horses, as one man flagged another came forward and leaped into his place. The use of horses was an extravagance for these men of the hills, except for the cumbersome beasts who were their pack-horses. She observed how close these Farrs lived to the earth, in harmony with it, and their communications were linked to an older race than the merchants and travellers who relied upon fast horses and wheels to transport themselves and their goods.

She felt a grudging admiration for their effortless grace as they descended to firm ground and were soon clattering along a lane that lead to the village of Laverock. The castle was not much larger than a hunting-tower and of pleasant aspect. Sadly she recalled that in different circumstances she might have been making this journey as a bride, this castle her home. She felt that she could have been happy here.

As they rode along the path, she saw gipsies everywhere, men and women working in the fields, singing as they tilled the land. A sudden gleam of sunshine shafted the castle, glistening on its walls like an omen of joy, and far above her head she heard the sweet deep-throated song of the mavis.

They entered the shadowy courtyard and a door opened. The woman who rushed out to greet them was clearly Mirella Farr, for she was unmistakably Dirk's mother, but young-looking, handsome still.

She curtseyed, considerably flustered. Obviously no one had told her to expect a royal visitor. "Your Majesty is most welcome."

A groom appeared, led Kirsty's horse to the mounting block. Dirk had disappeared among the servants awaiting orders. Trying to gain a little time, Kirsty rubbed her leg and groaned.

"Is something wrong, Your Majesty?" asked Mirella Farr.

Kirsty nodded. If only she did not have to walk!

"Saul, come here."

The blacksmith nodded and lifting Kirsty from her horse carried her across the courtyard, up a winding staircase to the guest chamber. He set her down in a handsome padded chair and Mirella bustled in after him. She knelt by Kirsty's side, placed a footstool before her. "I can assist Your Majesty, for I have some skill with unguents."

At that moment Dirk appeared in the doorway. Mirella turned, smiling, to greet him and then Kirsty was forgotten.

Mirella screamed, then rushed forward, tearing at her son's cloak. He groaned as she tried to remove it and stumbled towards the settle. He lay back and Kirsty saw that the doublet which had replaced the guard's uniform was not crimson as she had thought, but stained with blood.

Mirella chattered to him in Romany, obviously chiding him.

"All is well," he said weakly, "the purpose is served. My life or his. And we have our Queen safe."

He looked across at Kirsty, who crouched back in her chair in a very unqueenly fashion. Suddenly, with a curse, he pushed his mother aside and coming to Kirsty stared down at her. She turned her head away, but the deception was over. The movement of being carried up the narrow staircase had dislodged the Queen's auburn wig, which tilted at a dangerous angle. Even as Kirsty put up her hand, it tumbled to the floor and her own soft blonde hair cascaded to her shoulders.

Dirk stretched out his hand, raised the mask she still wore.

For the first time, Kirsty smiled. "Aye, my lord Laverock, you may curse as much as you like. You may do what you will with me, for the Queen is safe – in Hermitage."

The Queen was indeed safe, but considerably distressed still more in sorrow than in anger, at her apparent betrayal by her *Garde Ecossaise*.

"A trap, madam," Lord James said as he had stumbled back to the royal litter, "we must be gone with all haste."

Later he told her that Laverock had appeared and seized Howison. "He thought she was Your Majesty and he carried her off over the bridge to England."

"Could no one stop him?"

"Madam, there were only two of us."

"My poor Howison! I wonder where they are?"

Lord James and Bothwell exchanged glances. Neither wanted to confront the Queen with the unpleasant news that by now Howison was most likely to be the guest of the Queen of England. They shuddered to think of Elizabeth's rage – and its consequences upon Kirsty – when the imposture was discovered.

But Mary read the truth in their eyes. "I cannot believe it, I cannot. Oh James, you see what all this means? This meeting, I believed in it. So much depended thereon." She began to cry and they watched her mutely, unable to think of words which might bring comfort, for there were none.

Later she asked them: "You are certain that this villain was my lord Laverock. You say he was cloaked?"

"Cloaked, aye, but he did not try to disguise himself. He had even discarded his uniform," added James.

The Queen sighed. She had to admit that Dirk Farr was guilty, but still she hesitated, her hand poised over the order for Lord Laverock's arrest.

"The law gives no choice, madam," said James. He knew how foolish she was in matters of clemency to known criminals, how she had a soft heart towards sending any man to his death.

The Queen looked at him. The law said that any who laid hands upon the Queen's royal person suffered death. In Dirk Farr of Laverock's case, he would be executed and his lands forfeit to the Crown.

"You know where to find him?"

"Aye, madam. Word has come from my lord Bothwell. Farr and his gipsies have been seen heading towards Laverock."

The Queen nodded sadly. She had a strange feeling that her half-brother would rather enjoy taking Dirk Farr, whom he had never liked or trusted, scornful of her leniency and affection for one who was a known gipsy. She felt that Dirk Farr's fall from grace had given extra power to James, material for the future, that once he had warned her against Laverock and she had not heeded him.

She took the quill he had ready for her use.

"Very well, I will sign it. Go you to Laverock and bring my lord Laverock to Edinburgh on a charge of treason."

She watched him leave her presence, bowing, his air jaunty. She sighed. Mary of Scotland had a kind heart. She would miss Dirk Farr, who had brought a vagabond air of romance to her court.

She hoped James would not use his moment of triumph as an excuse for a blood-bath of the Clan Farr.

CHAPTER
TWELVE

At Laverock, through the long hours of the night, Mirella Farr fought to keep her son alive. He was weak from loss of blood, and his wound, a deep gash from a sword-thrust in his side, had been dressed. She had used all her cunning, her life-giving herbs, but he was already running a fever and he lay unmoving, pale as death.

Kirsty, wearing one of Mirella's kirtles over the Queen's petticoat, watched with her; the two women who had never met before, bound in the love each bore to the man who seemed to be slipping away from them.

Mirella and Kirsty talked little, but they learned from the gipsies what had happened. Mirella translated for Kirsty's benefit, and gradually she pieced together the story which clearly proved Dirk's innocence.

The Farrs had discovered through their very efficient secret society that Master Armstrong was plotting to abduct the Queen of Scots when she went forth to Kershopefoot to meet the English Queen. There were many in England who hated Mary as Elizabeth's rival and as a Roman Catholic. Master Armstrong had lured Dirk to a meeting and then ambushed him on the way to Hermitage. He had been wounded, stripped of his uniform and left for dead.

Fortunately the gipsies had found him, but as he had by then been unconscious for some hours, he had known that there was no time left to warn the Queen before she left Jedburgh for her meeting with Elizabeth. She would walk into a trap at Kershopefoot. Wounded as he was, near death, he knew the only chance lay in reaching the bridge before her.

Kirsty dried her tears. She was no better off knowing the truth. Nor did it help Dirk's cause, for Nigel Armstrong had escaped to England and unless he could be brought before Queen Mary and made to confess, there was no hope of proving his innocence, especially as he had abducted the "Queen" in her half-brother's presence.

The two women stared helplessly at the beloved face, so pale and still, knowing that escape for him was impossible. Had he not been gravely wounded, then he might with the Farrs' help have been smuggled out of the country. But his life-blood as it seeped away seemed to carry with it all will to fight, to survive.

Mirella tried to explain to Kirsty, who was weeping at her side. "To run away, to be for ever a fugitive is not the way of the Farrs, my child. We are fighters born but when we are defeated, then we accept the hand of destiny."

She did not further distress Kirsty by adding that gipsies shared, in common with other creatures of the wild, rules of life more in keeping with natural laws. A gipsy in captivity was quite capable of dying of no injury or apparent cause, but simply by rejecting the will to live.

Nor did she tell Kirsty that Dirk had recovered consciousness briefly and had whispered to his mother: "Promise you will not try too hard to keep me alive. If I am like to die anyway, better this way, comfortably here at Laverock, with the two I love best in all the world, than a traitor's death on the scaffold outside the Tolbooth."

Mirella found Kirsty in the kitchen and said: "My son is awake and would speak with you. Take care, for he is very weak."

Kirsty ran upstairs. Dirk lay against the snowy pillows, his eyes closed and even she could not pretend that it required a miracle greater than Mirella's herbs to save him now. At her approach his eyes fluttered open, he smiled wanly and as they clasped hands, for a little while they said nothing.

"Kirsty," he began at last.

"Nay, do not talk, I promised Mirella I would not tire you."

Her words brought back the ghost of his quizzical mockery. Then it faded and he sighed, "There is much to be said between us, and time is short. I would not wish to leave you with so many things unsaid. Ours has been a strange hand-fasting, and you have good reason to hate me."

How much the effort of speaking cost him, she thought in agony. "Hush," she said, trying not to weep, "I am to blame for your present sorry state. Had I told you directly at Kershopefoot that I was not the Queen, you might have made good your escape."

He shook his head. "It was already too late."

"Your wound could have been attended to earlier, at least you would not have had that dire ride ahead of you. I can never forgive myself!"

"Why did you not tell me?" There was no reproach in his voice, and when she looked away, he said: "Ah, I begin to see. You too, thought I was in the pay of Her Majesty's enemies in England."

"If I had known of Master Armstrong's duplicity, I would not—"

He looked at her. "Master Armstrong was high in your regard as well as in the Queen's. Would *you* have believed he was a villain? for no one else did."

She saw his eyelids were growing heavy and that talking had exhausted him. He took her hand again and holding it fast, fell asleep.

"Forgive me, my dearest," she whispered. But he made no sign that he heard her, and his breath laboured. Stroking his brow, kissing his unresponsive cheek, Kirsty longed to awaken him, longed to ask his forgiveness for the wrong she had done him. How greatly she loved him, she realised. If he died they would bury her heart in the grave beside him here at Laverock, for she would never love another.

Her vigil was interrupted by a distracted Mirella. "Lord James has arrived, with a troop of soldiers to arrest my son, to carry him to the Tolbooth on a charge of treason."

Lord James obviously did not trust Mirella, for she had hardly finished speaking than he was thrusting his way into the bedchamber, sword in hand.

Curtseying briefly, Kirsty cried: "See for yourself, my lord, he is sore wounded."

Lord James eyed Kirsty with contempt. "So you were part of this treason? I shall inform Her Majesty that I found you weeping at this traitor's bedside, and urge her to command your arrest."

"I care not what you do, my lord. For Lord Laverock is innocent, as I am also. Our only guilt is that we both loved the Queen too well." She faced him squarely. "I will willingly accompany Lord Laverock to the Tolbooth. We are guiltless of this crime – the plan to kidnap Her Majesty was Master Armstrong's—"

"Enough," he interrupted, "further lies will avail you nothing." He pointed to Mirella. "Woman, prepare your son to accompany me to Edinburgh."

Mirella shook her head. "My son is dying, surely you can see that, my lord? Should I try to do as you command, he will undoubtedly be dead even before he reached the gates of Laverock."

Lord James thrust her aside and stared down at the pale face on the pillows. He had seen many men with the marks of death about their countenances, and he did not doubt that this one also was not long for this world.

"Very well. I shall leave armed men to be stationed outside this door at all times. He shall remain here until such time as he is fit to go to Edinburgh."

Mirella knelt before him. "My gratitude, my lord."

He cut short her thanks, gnawing his lips. He recognised that the woman spoke truth and nervously hoped that Lord Laverock would live long enough to stand trial. In his present condition, to move him would mean his death long before they reached the Edinburgh road, and if he survived that distance, then the rough ride would certainly finish him off. And he did not want the easy way for Dirk Farr, death on the road: he wanted to see him condemned to die on the scaffold outside the Tolbooth. Lord James had a bloodthirsty streak. And it would also be useful as a lesson to his timorous half-sister, he thought, that it needed a man to rule Scotland, a man who could make decisions with his head and not his heart. Aye, Laverock's death on the scaffold would prove a fine reminder that she had been wrong about her most trusted servant, and a warning that she might make the same mistake again if she had not Lord James, with his superior judgement, as her counsellor.

Next morning, Kirsty tiptoed to Dirk's bedchamber, where his mother slept in a chair by the fire. She approached the bed with its still figure, almost afraid of what she would find. His face was white as the pillows, framed by rough black curls falling across his forehead. Nearer now, she saw the stubble of beard and that, mercifully, he still breathed.

The sight affected her greatly. How young and vulnerable he looked, with little resemblance to the strong, mocking, arrogant Dirk Farr she had despised! Now she wanted to gather him into her arms, and hold him against her heart, willing him to live. She sank down beside the bed, holding his hand and longing for his eyes to open so that she might see the bright fires burning in those crystal depths, which were like a mirror to the world. Look long enough, she thought, and she might see the whole pageant of life itself, past, present and future, in those clear depths.

Sadly she saw that his mind was far beyond the present, for there had been a deterioration during the hours of the night, as if the past already laid claim to him and the future carried him swiftly to the gates of death. What future? she thought. He had known at Jedburgh there was no future for them, and if he died now her own life would be bleak, for she would never cease to torture herself because she had deprived him not only of love but even of compassion. She could not even ask God's forgiveness for misjudging him.

One kiss and then she would go, she vowed, before Mirella awoke. One kiss.

His cheek was cold, and she touched his hair. As she did so a black curl wound itself around her finger and her heart ached with physical pain as she knew that this man so close to death was her beloved. Then through a blur of tears she saw that his eyes were open.

"What? Tears for me?" His smile was pale.

She held his hand tighter, unable to find words, and his returning grasp was firmer than she expected, as if he leaped into life at the sight of her.

"Are Lord James' guards still waiting?" She nodded and he smiled again. "Their patience will be rewarded. So be it. Once I said I would proudly die for my Queen, and now it seems I am to have that honour, one way or another. But for the wrong reason." He looked towards the window with its blue sky and scurrying clouds. "To die a traitor, for ever dishonoured, never to have the Queen know of my innocence."

Kirsty held his hands. " 'Tis my fault. If I had told you at the beginning that you were abducting the wrong person – if I had told you I was not the Queen—"

"Nay, Kirsty, your action led them away from Her Majesty, so you did indeed play your part in saving her. We were not safe until we reached the treacherous hillside. There among the pathways by the bogside which only the Farrs know, Armstrong and his men had no hope of catching us on their English horses."

"Surely you can explain to Her Majesty, beg for mercy?" Kirsty asked. "She is a kind and gentle lady, and thought well of you."

"She is also a queen, and queens play their part according to rules as well. There are the laws of the land which even they disobey at their peril." He sighed. "It is too late. Master Armstrong is no doubt safe back in England, and without him there is no means of proving my innocence."

"Was the English Queen implicated?"

"Only Master Armstrong could tell us that. All we know is that she never left Carlisle Castle. Almost certainly if any of this comes to light she will publicly disclaim all knowledge of a plot to abduct her 'dear cousin of Scotland'. All accusations will be dismissed as the ravings of a madman."

"Oh, Dirk – Dirk!" She buried her face in his neck. "I will talk to Her Majesty – and I will tell her. She must believe me. I cannot let you die."

He smiled and stroked her hair. "These are changed days! I had never thought to see you weep for me."

"I misjudged you – can you ever forgive me?"

" 'Twas my fault, for I deceived you." And he told her of his secret with the Queen, how he had arranged for her to go to Holyroodhouse into Her Majesty's service, because he wanted to watch over her. "Can you guess why?" he added gently. When she did not reply he said: "I have loved you since the first moment we met. And not because you look like the Queen, only because you are Kirsty Howison."

She sighed. "If ever we escape from this net which closes around us, I will prove that I love you too." She kissed him gently, but Dirk did not smile. He was pale and grave and she knew that he had plans of his own which he would not discuss with her, to cheat the executioner's sword. Not only had he lost blood but he had lost his spirit too, and she thought of the wild forest creatures in captivity who willed themselves to die when they were put in cages. If only there were some means to persuade him to live and to fight . . .

"I will be yours, my lord, handfasted – or whatever you wish," she whispered.

Sadly he shook his head. "It is too late, my love, too late for us."

"It is not. For I love you – with all my heart."

For a moment his voice quickened. "Do you? Then let us be wed – if I live – for that is my most earnest wish."

"And mine," Kirsty echoed, but it seemed a futile hope and dream.

Dirk slept after that, and Mirella remarked that his colour was better.

"I fear they will never take him alive," she added, weeping. "He will not die by the sword, for it is not in his destiny."

"How know you that?"

"It is in the cards. He will die here at Laverock." She sighed. "But I had thought that to be many years ahead."

Lord James was to return to Laverock within the week on his way back to Edinburgh with the Queen, for she was now fit enough to travel, recovered from the "New Influence", and longing for the comforts of Holyroodhouse after the draughty inhospitality of Hermitage.

Before Lord James was expected back, Kirsty went down to the little parish church, stern and unadorned, with niches on its ancient walls, hinting at its former faith. She found the minister in prayer and asked him to return with her to visit my lord Laverock. Requesting Mirella to accompany them to Dirk's bedchamber, she found him already dressed, albeit exhausted and pale, but awaiting the arrival of Lord James with quiet dignity and resignation.

"What is this, minister, surely not the last rites?" he asked tiredly.

The minister managed a bleak smile. "Nay, my lord, I understand that it is your wish – and this lady's – to be wed before your arrest. She feels there is some necessity of haste," he added uncomfortably, "since her good name is in jeopardy, having been handfasted to you for some time past."

"Handfasted?" Dirk smiled. "If Mistress Howison so desires, then I shall be happy to wed her. But leave us for a moment, sir."

The minister paused by the window. "As you wish, my lord, but I would point out that time is short. Already horsemen approach the castle."

"It must be Lord James," whispered Kirsty. "Let us hurry."

Dirk took her hands. "Not even Lord James would deprive a condemned man of his last wish to make honest his mistress." He shook his head. "I cannot allow you to do this, Kirsty, 'Tis too selfish a caprice of mine to have you as my wife."

"It is my wish too!"

"Nay, Kirsty, think sensibly upon it. I go to the Tolbooth and my part is swiftly over. You are at liberty to return to the Queen's service, to a good life, without a stain upon your character. The Queen will be proud to have you, a heroine who has suffered much rather than allow her to be endangered. But wed me and you face the Queen's displeasure, for then you carry my name and my dishonour."

"I care naught for that!" she protested. "I want only your love, I want only to prove your innocence. And if aught befell you—"

"Not if, Kirsty. What lies before me is inevitable."

"Then I shall spend the rest of my life proving your innocence."

Dirk looked at her in amazement. She seemed so strong and purposeful, and far from the obstinate girl he had first loved. He knew he could have absolute faith in her. If he went to a traitor's death, he knew she would do exactly as she said, carrying his name like a badge of honour until she proved to the Queen that he was innocent. He had found not only a woman worthy to be his wife and a member of the Clan Farr, but he had also found a king's daughter.

"This token of our marriage will prove to the Queen how greatly she wrongs you," she continued. "Besides, if you will not wed with me, my heart will break."

Gently he took her in his arms. There were kisses of compassion which had begun their story, kisses of anger and longing which had bruised her soul and left her body crying out for him. There were tender kisses, lover's kisses and now Kirsty's lips gave him hope and life and strength.

At the sound of horsemen in the courtyard below, she gently disengaged herself and ran to the window. "I think it is Lord James."

"Call the minister, then, if you are still of the same mind," Dirk said tautly.

" 'Tis not Lord James, 'tis Her Majesty – and Lord Bothwell!"

A few minutes later, the Queen entered the bedchamber and took Kirsty's hands. She looked pale and her voice was husky, but she was clearly recovered.

"Howison, *ma petite*, you did not come to any harm? God be thanked." Releasing Kirsty, she turned to look sternly at her *Garde Ecossaise*. "Nay, sir, do not rise, for they tell me you are sore wounded." Dirk saw the compassion in her eyes, even for the traitor she believed him to be. She sighed. "Well, Dirk Farr, what have you to say to your Queen before she takes you captive?"

Dirk bowed. "I am innocent, Your Majesty. I love you and have served you faithfully with all my heart. And I am prepared to die for you too, if such is your wish. If you believed that I had betrayed you, then I should not wish to live on dishonoured."

She smiled and knelt down beside his chair. "I bring you good tidings, Dirk Farr. My lord Bothwell must be thanked too, for he has been busy on your behalf, he and his Borderers. A few days ago they captured a *Garde Ecossaise* hiding in a disused peel tower; he said his name was Laverock and he had been wounded on the Queen's business. Bothwell's men did not believe him and tried him out with some words of Romany which he did not understand, which was strange indeed for a supposed member of the Clan Farr. They brought the man to Hermitage." She paused. "Have you guessed his name?"

"Nigel Armstrong, Your Majesty, for we had met and fought," Dirk said promptly.

She clapped her hands delightedly. "There now, did I not tell you?" she said to Bothwell. "My lord Laverock's innocence is confirmed."

"What transpired between you?" asked Bothwell.

"He waylaid me on the way to Hermitage, we fought, but I did not know that I had wounded him before he left me for dead and stripped me of my uniform."

"So be it," said Bothwell. A moment later he continued:

"Master Armstrong knew when we brought him to Hermitage that his enterprise had failed, and so had his plans to abduct Her Majesty and carry her over the border to sell her to her enemies in England. He swore that he was tired and had a fever, which was obvious to all of us. But he promised that next morning, after a night's rest, he would write out a full confession of his part in the plot, including the names of those who had employed him. There was one person we were

eager to know about, Her Majesty Elizabeth of England –
had she knowledge of this plan? Master Armstrong shook his
head. He could tell us no more that night, we were to wait
until the morn. But Elizabeth was guiltless, he said, when we
– insisted," he added grimly, "that we would allow him no
rest until that matter was clear. He told us that he had
invented the final details of the meeting for his own ends, and
those of the men who employed him in England. Elizabeth
had been informed that her 'dear sister' was delayed in
Edinburgh where the 'New Influence' was rife in the court.
Elizabeth is mortally afraid of illness of any sort, so she
decided to remain at Carlisle. Armstrong and his con-
spirators, prepared the litter to look as if they carried the
Queen."

"Has he then signed a confession?" asked Dirk.

"Nay, Laverock – and never will. Next morning we discovered he had hanged himself rather than implicate those in
the plot. The business is ended."

"I shall try and persuade my dear cousin to meet me when
she journeys north next summer," said Mary. Bothwell and
Dirk exchanged glances over her head. Surely she did not
believe that the wily Queen was completely innocent? Would
this guileless, trusting Mary never see dishonesty in anyone
until it was too late? She was smiling now at Dirk. "And what
have you to say before we take you captive?"

"Captive, madam? I have always been your captive."

"I mean, Dirk Farr, back into service as my personal
guard, if you can forgive us for doubting you. And this dear
lass of mine." She stretched out her arms to Kirsty. "If it had
not been for your courage in remaining silent, afraid as you
must have been, Master Armstrong's plan might well have
succeeded, but you led them away from us and gave us safe
return to Hermitage. You are truly a king's daughter, Kirsty
Howison. Remain here with Dirk Farr until he is fit to travel,
and then you shall both be with me in Holyrood."

Dirk intervened swiftly. "There is one small matter,
madam. Before your arrival, we were about to be wed. Kirsty
would have it no other way. If I were condemned, then she

wished to wear my dishonour in the name she would carry—"

"A wedding – a wedding, how delightful." And as Mary embraced Dirk and Kirsty, a shadow filled the doorway. "James, do come in and do not stand there scowling. We are staying at Laverock for a wedding. And I shall be matron-of-honour."

Weddings at the royal court and in noblemen's houses tended to be boisterous affairs; the couple wedded had to be publicly bedded. However, the bridegroom's recently endangered life preserved some shreds of modesty about the occasion. Her Majesty, however, insisted upon seeing them bedded and left them each sitting decorously against a bank of pillows in a bed and canopy strewn with wild flowers. This ritual satisfied, she departed with Lord Bothwell and Lord James to the wedding feast hastily prepared by Mirella and the Clan Farr.

As the door closed, Kirsty felt suddenly shy as she nestled at the side of her husband in the big soft bed. He kissed her gently at first, and then to her surprise she found that a wounded man was capable of considerable passion. For his lips sought hers in such hunger and love that they brought forth a longing for the day when she would truly be his wife in body as well as spirit.

"I love you," he said, "now and unto the world's end."

"And I love you."

And so they drew the curtains on this world that they had made together, small and secure against the night, then, arms entwined like sleeping children, they closed their eyes and waited in hope and faith for all the days that lay ahead.

Masquerade
Historical Romances

Intrigue excitement romance

ROSAMUND
by Julia Murray

Sir Hugh Eavleigh complies most reluctantly with the Earl of Carston's invitation to stay with him. What can it be, after all, but a clumsy attempt to snare him for the Earl's daughter, Lady Rosamund Daviot? But on his way to the Earl's residence, Sir Hugh is waylaid by a pair of highwaymen — one of whom proves to be the enchanting, scapegrace Rose, whom he can forgive but cannot forget.

It is not until his stolen watch is mysteriously returned to him that he realises that his Rose and Lady Rosamund are one and the same — and that they are embarked on a collision course with danger.

Masquerade
Historical Romances

**Intrigue
excitement
romance**

MOON OF LAUGHING FLAME
by Belinda Grey

Could Deborah forget her old, strict life in Victorian
England and become the obedient squaw of Adam-
Leap-The-Mountain — the arrogant half-breed brave
who was willing to kill to gain her?

THE ICE KING
by Dinah Dean

A season in St. Petersburg at the court of Czar
Alexander was Tanya's one chance of gaiety. Yet
she fell in love with Prince Nikolai — the Ice King —
a man of whom she knew nothing . . .

Look out for these titles in your local paperback shop from
11th January 1980

The Mills & Boon Rose is the Rose of Romance

Look for the Rose of Romance this Christmas

Four titles by favourite authors in a specially-produced gift pack.

THAT BOSTON MAN *by Janet Dailey*

MY SISTER'S KEEPER *by Rachel Lindsay*

ENEMY FROM THE PAST *by Lilian Peake*

DARK DOMINION *by Charlotte Lamb*

UNITED KINGDOM £2.20 net
REP. OF IRELAND £2.40

First time in paperback.

Still available from your local paperback retailer.

Masquerade
Historical Romances

Intrigue excitement romance

THE ABDUCTED HEIRESS
by Jasmine Cresswell

Georgiana Thayne was so determined not to be married for her money that she pretended to be plain and childishly stupid. It took an abduction by the wicked Marquis of Graydon to make her show her true colours . . .

RUNAWAY MAID
by Ann Edgeworth

Emphatically refusing Sir Joseph Varley, the suitor of her parents' choice, Miss Robina Westerley took her destiny into her own hands — and ran away. Rescue from the worst consequences of her impulsive action always seemed to come from the lofty, imperturbable Sir Giles Gilmore — yet how would they ever mean anything to each other, when he believed that Robina was only a lady's maid?

THE MARKED MAN
by Meriol Trevor

Claudine looked like an innocent schoolgirl, but she was prepared to shelter Gabriel — the infamous Marked Man — from the French Revolutionary soldiers who had invaded her beloved Luxembourg. She soon found that her heart was in greater danger than her life.

These titles are still available through your local paperback retailer